BLOOD LEGACY

WOLF MOON ACADEMY TRILOGY

JEN L. GREY

CHAPTER ONE

"Are you sure about this?" Kai's face was a mask of indifference, which wasn't normal. Instead of his brown eyes twinkling and wearing a smile on his face, it was as if I was nothing to him.

I'd hurt him in ways I wished more than anything that I could take back, but he wasn't my true mate. No matter how hard I had tried to forget about Liam, it never worked. Though, to be fair, Kai knew exactly what he'd been getting into. "Yes, they hurt my brother this past weekend, and Simon attacked me. I was barely able to defend myself." The four heirs to The Blood Council were a force to be reckoned with. When I first met them at a party, I had challenged them, and it was something that the four of them couldn't let go of at first. Simon was the main one still holding the biggest grudge against me, for not only the challenge but also for Liam completing our fated mate bond.

"Well, maybe if you didn't solidify your bond with Liam, you wouldn't have had that problem." His eyes flashed with hurt. "Things could've been different if you hadn't left the party with him."

"What did you expect me to do?" For the very first time, he was annoying me. I understood he was hurt, but he was being unreasonable. Liam's wolf had been in control, if I hadn't stepped in the way I had, things would've gotten much worse. Besides, there had been a group of humans in the house, watching everything go down. "Let him beat you, my brother, and Nate into a bloody mess? You know he still would've demanded that I go with him."

"That's the thing. You're stronger than you realize." Kai's voice got louder, and he paused, glancing around the gym.

"Maybe I didn't realize it because my trainer was holding me back." I'd been asking him when the physical training part kicked into gear. Even Coach Riley said something a few weeks ago, but Kai swore up and down that I wasn't ready, which also meant Gertrude got held back with me. "How could I have challenged Liam when I don't know how to stand strong against him?"

"He wouldn't have hurt you." His eyes widened as he realized what he'd just said.

He admitted that Liam cared, which was opposite of the point he was trying to drive home now. "Kai, I didn't mean to hurt you. You're one of my closest friends." I wanted to say if Liam wasn't in the picture, things would have been different. Somehow, I stopped myself. That wasn't fair to him or Liam. At the end of the day, Liam is who and what I wanted, and he now felt the same way about me.

"Stop." His eyes flashed with warning or hurt. At the moment, I wasn't entirely sure. "We aren't doing this here," he said in a low voice as he pointed around the gym.

I glanced around the rows of free weights and various machines used for all kinds of exercising. To the left was a room filled only with mats where the coach was training Tripp and Barry.

"Doing what?" Gertrude came out of the girls' locker room and walked past a few people who were using the machines, lifting weights.

Kai had been assigned as our trainer over the past month and a half for our Tuesday and Thursday Shifter Endurance class, but he wasn't pushing us hard at all. After Simon had attacked me and my brother this past weekend, I realized that I needed to focus on fighting as well. If there was one thing I'd learned since coming here, it was that the heirs were out for themselves and they'd take out anyone they felt was a threat or got in their way.

"She's wanting to skip weights and learn combat." Kai ran a hand through his messily styled hair and sighed.

"Oh, I'm down!" She clapped her hands as she bounced on her feet, making her blonde hair bob. "Those other two," she said as she pointed at the room with all of the mats and the other guys doing their training, "have been doing that since day one. It's about damn time we get in on some action."

Wow, I didn't think I'd ever seen her smile before. "See." Kai and I had to act normal now that Gertrude was here. "She wants the same thing."

"Fine, but let's go outside to do it since they already *claimed*," Kai emphasized the word, "that room." He pointed to the room that really only had space for one set of fighters.

Yeah, that was a low blow. He might be trying to be subtle. Though he obviously had to be alluding to the fact that Liam and I solidified our bond this past weekend prior to Max being taken hostage. I had to be the bigger person and rise above his snide remark.

The three of us headed outside and neared the woods that surrounded most of the school. Kai frowned as he stopped at a grassy area that was about fifty feet from the gym and a hundred yards from the academics building. He then turned to face us. "I guess first, we'll need to practice blocking."

"Really? Blocking?" Gertrude rolled her eyes. "We need to focus on offense, not defense."

"Look, do you want to learn or not?" Kai's voice had a little bit of a growl in it.

He most definitely wasn't acting normal.

"The reason you aren't getting trained properly is because of coddling." A deep, sexy voice sounded from behind me.

My heart began to race, and I turned around to see my handsome mate heading my way. His blue eyes were almost as dark as his short dark brown hair, and his muscular build seemed more tense than usual. He wore the customary Wolf Moon uniform with a blood-red polo shirt and khaki pants.

The intimidating eastern heir to The Blood Council flanked him as they swaggered in our direction.

"Holy shit." Gertrude looked at me and then back to Liam. "I knew you smelled different, but I didn't realize it was due to him."

Before I could respond, Liam pulled me into his arms and kissed my lips. *You're always around him.*

Behave. I pulled back, trying to keep our displays of affection limited so they wouldn't hurt Kai further. *He's a good friend.*

He wants to be more than that. His jealousy filtered through the bond.

It never would've been like that if you'd manned up in the very beginning, so stop. I stepped out of his arms and glanced at Evan. "What are you doing here?"

"Liam has asked me to step in and train you." Evan's skin was pale, which was rare among shifters, and his gray eyes were so light they could easily be mistaken as white. Between that and him being built like a freaking Ford truck, he was scary as hell. He took off his school jacket, revealing a Wolf Moon Academy standard silver tank top paired with blood-red shorts. The muscles in his arms were almost as big as his head.

"She's mine to train." Kai's jaw clenched.

"Not anymore." Liam wrapped his arm around my waist, pulling me closer. "She'll be trained by one of our own."

"Our own?" Kai arched an eyebrow and chuckled without humor. "So, now she's good enough to be an elite? You do realize my father works for you, so I'm technically ranked higher than her."

Shit, they were having a pissing match. *What are you doing? I have a class. You can't come in here and just pull me out of it.*

Actually, I can. He nodded to Evan. "He's training her from here on out, which means blondie here is all yours." He pointed at Gertrude. "It'll be good for you to focus all of your attention on her anyway."

"Let me guess—you got Daddy's approval for this change." Kai closed his eyes and shook his head. "I should've seen it coming."

"Maybe it wouldn't have happened if you'd actually trained her. Plus, she wouldn't have gotten hurt." Evan's voice was deep and rough.

"What injury?" Some of the gusto seemed to leave Kai.

"I feel so lost." Gertrude cleared her throat and took a breath. "I'm going to run and get some water." She headed back toward the gym.

When no one answered, Kai took a step toward me and looked me over. "Are you hurt?"

"I'm almost healed." I unconsciously rubbed the shoulder that Simon had sunk his teeth into.

"What happened?" Kai's eyes landed right where my hand touched. He approached me, holding out his hand to touch me.

"No." Liam stepped in between Kai and me. "Don't touch her."

"Really? How the hell do you expect him," Kai said as he pointed his finger at Evan accusingly, "to train her without any touching, especially if she's his only student?"

"Because he won't be around to watch." Evan's voice was deep and commanding.

"Like hell, I won't be." Liam turned around and glared at his friend.

Oh, dear God. "He's right." Liam couldn't be there, and to be honest, I was surprised that he wanted to be. I had a feeling that training was going to be rough and hands-on, and we were newly mated. As newly claimed mates, we were still getting acclimated to the bond. Since he'd fought ours so hard at first, it was taking an even harder toll on him. It didn't help that he was used to always getting everything he wanted, but this time he was going to have to let go. I needed Evan.

"See, I knew she'd want me there." Liam's cocky grin spread across his face.

"No, Evan's right." I turned and faced Liam. It was going to be a stand-off. "You won't be around."

"Now's not the time to try to be funny." Liam scowled at me.

"I'm not being funny." Every ounce of me knew I needed this even if it was going to be difficult and painful.

This past weekend, I'd learned that my biological father was the Overseer of the original Blood Council and had been killed nineteen years ago. I was raised by a man who treated me as his own. Hell, I had always thought I was his blood; that's how damn good he was to me. Despite that, he didn't have elite status. "You weren't there that night to protect me, and it could happen again. I need to be able to not only stand my ground in a fight but win."

"She's right, and you know it." Evan nodded his head, and, dare I hope, just maybe I saw approval shine in his eyes.

"So, you're okay with this?" Kai pinched the bridge of his nose and took a deep breath. "He's going to beat the ever-loving shit out of you."

"No, I won't." Evan glared at Kai. "But I won't treat her like she's weak because she's a female. When she's in a fight, a male isn't going to go, oh wait. I won't kill her or hit quite as hard. They won't give a fuck, just like Simon."

Kai's shoulders deflated, and his forehead creased. "To be with someone who will always make you a target? To have to learn how to fight and defend yourself? To never know who is really friend or foe? That's what you want?"

The problem was that, even if I didn't want all that, fate had other plans. What no one except Liam, Mom, Dad, and Max now knew was that I was the rightful heir to the overseer position, which was essentially the same as the President of the United States in the shifter world. If that wasn't enough, fate had decided to make Liam, the heir to The Blood Council's north member seat, my true mate. I had no choice but to accept my role before someone tried to kill me again. "Yes ... I need to be able to rely on myself. Sometimes, we have to be our own saviors."

"She's already made her choice, so leave it alone." Liam's voice was raspy as he tried to rein in his wolf.

"You kind of forced her into it." Kai frowned as he looked at me. "Mia, I hope you don't regret this."

"I'm not sure how much clearer she can be unless you meant that as a threat." Liam narrowed his eyes at Kai.

Quit it. Right when I thought things might calm down. He added more fuel to the fire.

"Of course not. I'm not you." Kai spat the words.

"Is there a problem?" Mr. Hale appeared right behind our little group.

The four of us turned in his direction.

Liam's father stood there, wearing a suit that fit his trim figure perfectly. He looked like an older version of Liam. The more council members I saw, the odder it was. They all appeared to be so much younger than they actually were. Yes, shifters had great genes, but it was like theirs were on steroids. They looked more like older siblings than parents.

"Nope, we were just informing Kai of the trainer change." Liam crossed his arms as he glanced at Kai. "It's not going over well."

"Didn't think it would." Mr. Hale chuckled. "That's why I'm here." His blue eyes, only a shade darker than Liam's, glanced at me. "Ms. Davis, you sure do seem to cause a lot of problems." His mouth spread into a smile, but it didn't reach his eyes.

He must still be annoyed with me. "Never intentional."

"But trouble all the same." Mr. Hale pointed at Kai. "Get back inside and train the others. I'm sure Coach Riley could use some help."

"Yes, Sir." Kai huffed and glared one last time at Liam before jogging back to the gym.

"He's going to cause trouble too." Mr. Hale tsked and

shook his head. "Which is a shame. I'll have to call his father."

"No, he won't." Kai was a good person, just hurting. I hadn't been able to see him prior to today with my brother being hurt by Micah and Simon plus getting him settled back in at home to heal. Max had stayed at Wolf Moon Academy's dorm all day Sunday. Monday, we took him home to our parents where he found out the whole truth and why he'd gotten hurt. Luckily, he'd felt the same way as I did. We were still a family, and knowing who my real father was didn't change anything even though both of us were conflicted. So, Kai hadn't been a priority. "He's just... going through things?" I didn't mean for it to sound like a question.

"Well, he better figure it out sooner rather than later," Liam grumbled as he took my hand in his.

"You need to put him in his place." Mr. Hale arched an eyebrow at Liam before his attention turned back to me. "So, Mia, as you probably have heard, you are now being trained by Evan."

I nodded and took a gulp. I was kind of scared of what kind of training Evan would put me through, but it was something that needed to be done.

"Evan's the strongest, at least physically, of the four heirs. You two run off and start." He turned his attention to Evan. "I need to talk to Liam alone."

"Yes, Sir." Evan bowed his head ever so slightly and walked over to me, touching my shoulder. "Let me see what your wound looks like."

Liam growled.

"Stop being an ass." I moved my shirt so he could see my skin. It was pretty much healed, but it was still sore and scabbed over from where Simon had sunk his teeth in.

"I think we should wait until Thursday to begin." He dropped his hands and took a step back. "It's still not healed enough for extensive training."

"That's fine." Mr. Hale waved him off. "You two head on out."

"She can stay here if she wants." Liam stood tall.

"No, she can't." Mr. Hale lifted his chin, and power rolled off his body. "I'm still in charge, not you. At least, not yet."

It's fine. The last thing I wanted to do was to come between him and his parents. *Meet me back at the dorm when you're done.*

It won't be long. He leaned over and kissed my cheek.

Mr. Hale sneered as he watched his son's actions toward me. "Oh, and Ms. Davis, I'll be expecting to see you tomorrow in the restaurant for coffee at noon. Don't be late." The animosity in his voice was clear.

If I had thought he might have been accepting of me, all that hope vanished. He looked at me with pure disgust. Mr. Hale was the reason I was at Wolf Moon. Bree had told him about how I stood up to the heirs at a party and that there was something about me. He'd paid for my first year here for two reasons. The first was that he didn't want anyone to have any effect over Liam, and two, he was intrigued by my wolf's strength. At first, he was ecstatic about me being here and even mentioned mentoring me for a city alpha position. Despite that, when he learned I was his son's fated mate, he wanted me gone. The closer Liam and I became, the more Mr. Hale's dislike of me grew.

It couldn't be a good thing when a council member wanted you gone.

CHAPTER TWO

W hen I walked into the dorm, I found Bree on the sofa, crying, her long dark brown hair cascading over her shoulders as she cried into her hands. Her face jerked up, and her blue eyes widened when she saw me there. "What ... What are you doing here? You have class."

I was just going to ignore that since she was deflecting. "Hey, what's wrong?" I hurried past the first hallway on the left, which led to my bedroom, and sat down next to her.

The dorm was the nicest place I'd ever lived. Our room was on the top floor, which was reserved for the council's family. The walls were painted the silver of our school's logo, which made the rooms feel larger. The room was furnished with a recliner on either side of the blood-red leather couch and a huge flat screen on the wall across from the sofa. Our kitchen was in the corner of the room with partial walls that kept the rooms somewhat separated.

"It's nothing." She sniffed and wiped a tear away from her face.

"It sure doesn't look like nothing." I didn't want to pressure her, but she needed to know I was there for her.

"Well, it's Nate." Her bottom lip pouted a little. "He's wanting me to come home to meet his parents over fall break, but I can't."

"Why not?" To me that sounded like a very good thing. He was ready to take their relationship to the next level.

"Don't you remember who my parents are?" She placed her hands in her lap. "They are pissed about Liam and you. Could you imagine how they would take news of Nate? I can't bring that into our relationship. I can't ask that of him."

"But it's his choice to make. You don't have the right to make the decision for him." That's what Liam had done with us. He decided on his own that I wouldn't want to take all the risks of becoming a council mate. I'd be a target for anyone that wanted to hurt him, but the thing was, he was worth the risk. "Look at how that worked out with your brother."

A small smile spread across her face, and she leaned over to wrap her arms around me. "I am so lucky to have you in my life."

"I love you too." I hugged her back. "I'm thinking you don't plan on leaving him, right?"

She pulled back and frowned. "I know I'm supposed to, but... I can't."

"Honestly, there is absolutely no reason why you should." Yes, it was clear that the council thought fated mates made them weak, but I didn't agree. Destiny had to know something we all didn't. In my case, I was meant to be the Overseer, so it made sense that Liam and I were meant to be. "It's something I hoped the heirs changed when they take over." Hell, I'd be taking over with them, and I'd make sure it changed.

"You really think there is hope?" Her eyes lit up as she anticipated the next words out of my mouth.

"If I have anything to do with it, there will be." Nate was the perfect half to her. He was amazingly kind and treated her like gold. That was what mates were meant to do; make you strong and complete. After everything we'd been through, finally, Liam was coming around.

If the both of us could handle the pressure of the council, there was nothing that could get in our way.

"Then, I'll tell him yes." A small smile spread on her face. "I'll come up with something to tell Dad." She waved her hands around.

The front door swung open as Liam entered the room. His face was tense, and his jaw ticked, which was a sign of him being royally pissed off.

"I take it things didn't go well?" There was always such turmoil around and involving the two of us. I hated that we couldn't just be happy.

"No, but he'll learn to deal with it soon." He walked over to pull me to my feet and into his arms.

"Dad?" Bree stood beside us and arched an eyebrow.

"Yeah, he wants me to reject her." He ran his fingers through my hair. "I told him he could go to Hell."

"I never thought I'd see the day when you would challenge the council." She headed toward her room. "I have a feeling I don't want to see what comes next." She slammed her door.

As soon as we were alone, his lips were on mine.

It bothers me that I'm causing so many problems for you. Even as I said the words, his lips were making goosebumps climb my skin.

You've made me the happiest I've ever been, and I'm not giving you up. He grasped my waist, lifting me up, not missing a beat while continuing to hold our kiss.

I wrapped my legs around his waist as he headed to my

bedroom. Within seconds of slamming the door shut with his arm, he was on top of me on my bed.

He placed his hands on the blood-red comforter on top of my bed to hold himself up and kissed down my neck, scraping his teeth against where he'd already marked me. One hand slipped under my shirt, and I raised myself slightly as he pulled it from my body.

I winced as my shoulder twinged with pain from the movement.

"Dammit, I tried to be careful." He threw my shirt on the ground, and his eyes zeroed in on my injury. It was only scabbed on the surface, but the tissue Simon had bitten through was still healing internally.

"It's fine. I'll be healed by tomorrow or Thursday." I lifted up and kissed his lips, wanting to get his focus back on me. He'd refused to have sex with me until I was better, so this wasn't going to go in my favor if I didn't get his attention elsewhere.

"Then, we can wait until then." He started to pull away from me, but I wrapped my legs around his waist, forcing his body forward.

He caught himself at the last second, trapping me within his arms.

"No, not allowed. You don't get to deny me this morning." I pushed him over and rolled on top of him. My lips slammed onto his, and I reached down, rubbing my hand along him over his pants.

I never thought I'd enjoy being dominated, but dammit, it turns me on. His hands wrapped around me, easily unclasping my bra. I removed it, tossing it over the side of the bed.

He raised his hips as he unbuttoned his jeans and removed them and his boxers in one movement. Within seconds, he was peeling the rest of my clothes away, removing all barriers from between us.

As I sat straight up, I guided him inside, and soon we were moving in synchronized movements. It had only been days, but it felt like a lifetime since we'd connected like this. The last time had been the night we claimed one another.

He sat up, brushing his lips against my breasts, making my head dizzy with more desire. I upped the pace, and within seconds, pleasure exploded throughout my core.

A low growl sounded from his chest as he rolled me over so he was settled on top. "Now, my turn," he said, his breath hitting my face.

Then, he thrust, hitting just the right spot once again.

I wrapped my arms around him, digging my fingernails into his back. He groaned with pleasure as he began moving harder and faster.

It wasn't long before both of us moaned in pleasure, connecting us in both mental and physical forms.

When it was all over, he plopped beside me and wrapped me in his arms. *I love you.*

My heart picked up a beat. He'd never said those words to me before even though I knew he felt them. His admission rang clear between us. *I love you too.*

Then, my eyes grew heavy, and I drifted off to sleep.

THE NEXT MORNING, Liam walked me to Pre-Calculus.

"I better get going to class." He lowered his lips to mine, kissing me almost borderline inappropriate for the hallways.

"See you soon." I winked and turned on my heel, heading into the classroom, Tripp's jade eyes met mine.

"Someone looks awfully happy." He gave me a sad smile. "Especially now that Kai is hurting."

That wasn't fair. "You knew Liam was my true mate." I met Tripp the same day I had met Kai. We were both freshmen getting a tour from an older academy student. So, to say Tripp became friends with both Kai and me at the same time wasn't an understatement. "It's not like I'd asked Liam to show up that night. I had intended to be with you all the entire night."

"You still could have tried harder." The corner of Tripp's eyes tightened. "I really thought you'd be more considerate than you were."

"I tried to make it work with Kai, but the bond is kind of overwhelming. I couldn't keep lying to myself or lead Kai on anymore. If you ever meet your fated mate...you will understand." If he thought I was going to let him get away with being an ass, he was wrong. I didn't deserve this. In fact, I had been struggling with how I felt and cared about both Liam and Kai just as bad, if not worse, when all this shit went down.

He sighed. "Maybe." He shook his head and glanced at the front of the class. The happy-go-lucky friend I knew wasn't here. "But at the end of the day, Kai is hurting. Maybe you do deserve your fated mate...but don't forget all the ones who got hurt along the way."

"If you're expecting me to apologize, it's not going to happen. I hate that Kai is hurting and that you are stuck in the middle, but I can't deny fate." I unzipped my bag and pulled out my notebook. "The problem is you're only seeing Kai's side and not putting my best interest at heart. It's great to know I had such a good friend. I won't make that mistake again."

His body tensed as he kept his eyes glued to the front of the class.

"Looks like there's some drama in paradise." Robyn flipped her red hair over her shoulder and glanced from one of her friends to the other. "This might be an interesting class today."

I hated those three with a passion. They were the other students who'd joined Tripp and me on the tour. We'd all shifted to run behind the school so Kai could show us the areas we were free to use. They had rushed back and poured skunk piss all over my clothes.

Before I could reply, Professor Walker breezed into the classroom, ending the conversation.

LATER, when I walked out of Comp one, I was a little surprised not to find Liam there, waiting for me. Maybe something came up.

I took the back stairwell, and as I walked through the door, a voice at the bottom stopped me in my tracks.

"Amber, how much clearer do I need to be?" Liam's voice was low and angry.

"You've got to be kidding me." A girl's voice raised. "You know both me and Dad were banking on you mating with me."

"Well, it's not going to happen." His voice was clear like he was making sure to enunciate each word. "I'm already taken."

"Liam, we can still salvage this."

Oh, hell no. I headed down the stairs, and when I turned the corner, blondie came into view. *Is this why you didn't meet me outside my classroom?*

Dammit, I'm sorry. He turned, and his blue eyes landed on mine. *I had a problem come up.*

That's an awful pretty problem. I wasn't jealous, but the girl was gorgeous. Her blonde hair was long and straight, and the girl rocked our school uniforms. She somehow managed to turn a plain button-down shirt sexy. She even had her skirt pulled up high enough that there was little left to the imagination. She was the same girl Liam had used to taunt me after we kissed for the first time right here in this stairwell, heading for the same class I was going to now. He'd had her plastered against him, allowing her to rub her fingers all over his chest.

The bitch needed to get a clue and fast.

Liam made his way over to me as I took the last step and grabbed my hand.

"Wait." The girl's aquamarine eyes widened. "This is who you dumped me for?"

What now? He had a girlfriend?

"We weren't dating; it was more of a business arrangement. You knew that as much as I did." Liam pulled me closer. *She didn't and doesn't mean anything to me.*

"Business arrangement?" What did that even mean? It was insane how they thought of mates as assets and not as actual soulmates. Something was really wrong with these people.

"Of course, he didn't tell you." She rolled her eyes and ran a hand through her immaculately styled hair. "We were engaged."

Whoa, what? Please tell me she's joking. I wanted to pull my hand from his, but it would give her too much satisfaction.

"No, we weren't." His eyes landed on mine. "We'd talked about it in the future after college. Then we broke up because well, hell, she was already showing me rings to buy her." *She meant nothing to me.*

"My dad is a regional alpha who reports to Mr. Croft." She paused and stuck her nose in the air. "You know, the council member representing the south. Obviously, I need to spell all this out for you ... especially since you don't know your place, but Liam will wake up soon."

"In case you didn't see the bite marks, he's mine, so back the fuck off." All of these entitled people were really pissing me off. Though, my role was getting clearer every day. When I took my place on the council, these assholes were going to have one hell of a rude awakening. I'd make sure of it. I had to be strong, not only for Liam but for myself. "It's a sealed deal, so why don't you take your skanky ass away from us."

Her plump bottom lip stuck out. "This is who you chose to be your mate?"

"Yup, the one and only." He bent down and brushed his lips against mine. "She's my fated mate, the love of my life."

"But we would've benefited each other greatly." She stomped her foot a little, placing a hand on her hip. "And the sex wasn't bad."

She was trying to hurt me and get me riled up. Her obvious goal was to cause us problems. "Well, at least you have those memories to keep you warm at night while I'm the one who is under him."

I love you so much. His words echoed in my ear as his shoulders shook ever so slightly. "Hmm ... Sometimes I'm under you."

"That's pretty mind-blowing too." I winked at him.

"You've made a horrible mistake." She opened the door to head out. "I'll just have to get with Evan or Simon, then."

She paused as if she was waiting for Liam to beg her to stay or say that he had changed his mind.

"Evan won't be interested. He warned me a while ago that you were a little too ambitious." Liam turned toward her and shrugged. "Simon would be down for a lay a time or two. Good luck with that."

She didn't even bother to respond but rather slammed the door behind her.

"You didn't think to tell me about a crazy ex?" I arched an eyebrow as he pulled me into his strong arms.

"It was nothing." He leaned his forehead against mine and took a deep breath. "She wasn't into me, not really. Only the power of what my future title would hold."

"You know that's also the only reason I'm in this." I had to tease him. We hadn't had time to just be two people who were into each other. We either had someone fighting the bond or a crazy heir trying to kill one of us. "Damn ... It better be worth it."

The corners of his mouth tilted up into one of the most genuine smiles I'd ever seen on him. Hell, I wasn't quite sure if I'd ever seen him smile before that moment; it almost took my breath away. Honestly, he always looked like he had the weight of the world on his shoulders.

"Is that so?" His fingers began to dig into my waist.

A giggle escaped before I could rein it in, which only encouraged him further.

"Stop." The words were only a breath as I collapsed into his arms in a fit of laughter. "Please, stop?"

"Fine, but only because you asked so nicely."

One of the doors opened from above the stairs, and I glanced at my watch. "Shit, I need to get to class. I want a minute to talk to Tripp."

"Fine, but he better behave himself. I'd hate to have

another person next to Kai on my list." He opened the door for me, and we hurried out into the hallway. "Are you sure you don't want me to go with you to meet with Dad? I can skip my class."

"No, he wants to talk to me alone. It's safer in the restaurant since there are a lot of people." When we reached my classroom, I stopped. "It'll be fine. I'll link you if it gets too bad."

"Promise?" He leaned down and kissed my lips.

"Promise."

I turned to walk into the room when Liam grabbed my arm. "Meet you back at your dorm at one?"

"You bet."

As I headed into the classroom, Tripp's jade eyes met mine, and he had a frown on his face.

Luckily, I got to class just in time for Mr. Johnson to stroll through the door and place his bag onto the floor underneath the whiteboard.

He wore his usual blood-red polo shirt and ran a hand through his thick black hair. He was at least in his sixties and had taught this class for the last twenty years.

"Good morning, everyone." He stood in front and eyed each one of us. "Let's get going."

I'd always enjoyed this class, but I had a feeling I'd wish it would last longer today for other reasons. I had to meet Mr. Hale right after this and had a feeling it wasn't going to be pleasant.

CHAPTER THREE

Not wasting any time, I stood as soon as class was over and hurried out the door. I didn't want to have another confrontation. I was hurt too, needing some time and space. It didn't help that I had to meet Mr. Hale.

"Mia, wait," Tripp called after me, but I didn't slow down.

I didn't have the time or energy to waste on him. If he felt bad for what he'd said, good. He should.

A hand touched my shoulder, gently turning me around, bringing us face to face.

He frowned as the fall breeze picked up though he had so much gel in his blond hair, it didn't budge. "I didn't mean to be a dick back there, but Kai is hurting so damn much."

"And you think that I'm not?" Yes, I was happy with Liam, but that didn't mean I didn't have regrets.

"You sure had a huge smile on your face when you walked into the room." He arched an eyebrow as if he was daring me to counter it.

"I may be happy with Liam, but that doesn't mean that I don't regret how things went with Kai." Right now, I had to get to Mr. Hale. If I was late, I could only imagine how much worse the meeting would be. "You knew just as well as him that Liam was my fated. Yet, you blame me for that night when he was about to lose control of his wolf. Yes, I wanted to try to be with Kai, but it wasn't possible. So instead of being happy for me that Liam and I worked things out as fate wanted, you are trying to make me feel like I owe you and him something. Frankly, you can kiss my ass. I don't have any more time to keep rehashing the same damn conversation." I turned on my heel and headed to the restaurant.

He didn't call after me, which was a good thing. I wasn't quite sure what would've happened if he forced the conversation more. We'd said all we had to say to one another.

When I got to the door, I took a deep breath. I had to calm my ass down before going inside. I had to be calm, cool, and collected while talking with Mr. Hale. Unlike Tripp, who was blunt and honest, this meeting was going to be all about strategy and who knew what else.

As I stepped into the restaurant, I wasn't surprised to find Mr. Hale already there. He was sitting in a corner booth on the left side of the restaurant. He'd chosen a table away from everyone else and waved his hand at me.

I walked past the various large rectangular and small circular tables placed strategically inside. It was strange that some called this a cafeteria. It was equivalent to a medium scale restaurant with waiters and waitresses attending to your every need.

As I slid into the seat across from him, a forced smile filled his face.

He had wanted to be the first one here so I would be approaching him. He had control of the situation by picking the booth, and I glanced at the table to find that he had already ordered my latte. He was doing everything in his power to show he was the one in charge.

"Well, hello, Ms. Davis." He glanced around as if expecting Liam to join us. He adjusted his blood-red tie that contrasted nicely with his black suit and a silver button-down shirt.

"I told him not to come." Mr. Hale was one of the few people who knew what had happened to my father. I had to keep my head on straight even if I wanted to reach out and smack him.

"And you think he'll listen to you?" Mr. Hale leaned back in his seat as his eyes settled on me.

"I think he'll respect me." From what I could tell, he didn't understand that concept. Hell, Liam was only starting to comprehend it. The Blood Council only understood fear.

"That's an interesting word to use." He lifted his coffee cup and took a sip. "Sometimes respect can be overrated."

"Oh, really?" I hated to admit that I was curious.

"Fear is how you keep people in line." He placed his cup back on the table and arched an eyebrow at me. "Why do you think Simon threatened and injured your brother?"

"Because he's a self-absorbed asshole." The words tumbled out before I could stop them. "Him only thinking of himself isn't a good trait to have if he's supposed to be sitting on the council in the next few years." My words were a challenge.

"Fear is a necessity of the council." His words were tense, and his blue eyes took on a slight glow. His wolf was coming out, not wanting me to question him any further.

Although being passive wouldn't get me answers. "How so? If the council is supposed to be advocating for the best of all, then wouldn't you want to be respected?"

"This, right here," he said as he slammed his palm on the table, "is the reason why you aren't right for my son. You're filling his head with possibilities that will ruin the very foundation that we stand on."

"And what foundation is that?" I hated to argue with Liam's dad, but it was clear that he wouldn't accept me as family. Obviously, he had only been okay with mentoring me when he thought he could control my position and who I reported to.

"One where everyone knows that the council knows best." He stared into my eyes as if expecting me to submit.

"Everyone has flaws and makes mistakes." I held his gaze, not diverting my attention elsewhere. I wanted him to know I couldn't be intimidated, which was clearly what he was trying to do. "We need to make it where people can talk to us and open our eyes to our own biases."

"We are strong leaders." He leaned across the table, his voice fading so low it was barely a whisper. "We know what's best for everyone."

"Then what's the point of the regional alphas or even the district alphas?" I refused to cower to him. If he saw fear, he'd strike.

He huffed and leaned back in his seat. His face turned a slight shade of red, but he paused a few seconds before talking. "We're obviously not getting anywhere, so let's cut to the chase."

I had no clue where this would go. "I figured this conversation was leading somewhere."

"What would it take to make you go away?" He huffed and straightened his black suit jacket.

"Do you mean for me to leave the school or Liam?" There was nothing in this world that would keep me from either, but I was curious about how he thought this would play out.

"Both." He pulled out a checkbook and laid it on the table. "You tell me the amount, and I'll make it happen."

Is everything okay? Liam's voice entered my mind. *I can't even decipher what your feelings are projecting right now.*

Your dad is trying to buy me off. I couldn't help the laughter that leaked through my words. *He has a blank checkbook sitting on the table, asking me what it'll take for me to leave.*

Are you fucking serious? His tone was low... almost deadly. *I'm heading that way.*

No, don't. When it was all said and done, I didn't want to put more of a strain on their relationship.

He's gone too far. Liam waited a moment. *I get that you want to talk to him alone, but we're a team. Right?*

He sounded slightly paranoid at the end. *If you're worried I'm going to take the money and run, I wouldn't do that.* He seemed apprehensive. *If you want to be here, then so be it.*

Leaving class now. I'll be there soon.

"Mia?" Annoyance was clear in Mr. Hale's tone.

"Sorry, Liam linked me." I grabbed my latte and took a sip. "He's on his way now."

"I thought he respected you too much to show." A small smile played at the corners of his mouth.

"We agreed together that he should come." I put my drink back on the table. I usually loved the taste, but right now, it could've been soured milk, and I wouldn't know the difference. "So, let me be clear. There is no amount of money in the world that would get me to walk away from Liam or this school."

"That can't be true." Mr. Hale pulled at the knot of his blood-red tie. "Everyone has a price."

Maybe most people did, but I had three very good reasons why my ass was staying put. The first and most important was Liam. I would never want to live my life without my fated beside me. Yes, it might have been possible. Look at my mom and my dad. They both had lost their fated and found another chance at love even if it wasn't even close to being the same. They still had each other.

Secondly, I was determined to unveil what had happened to my biological dad. I understood that it wouldn't bring him back, but his death never received justice. For him to leave and meet with the four council members, never to return, made me certain they at least knew something about it.

And lastly, I was going to take back what was rightfully mine. The council was created to have an overseer to help balance out the power. A majority vote of any council member's ideas was then presented to the overseer to either approve or reject. Right now, the council was able to push anything through without another set of independent eyes on it.

"Your son means more to me than any dollar amount you can jot down there." Seriously, who wrote checks anymore? For them to be all superior, you'd think they would at least know how to send a wire.

"You do realize that we're talking millions here." He tapped his finger on the checkbook like that might change my mind. "There truly is no amount off the table." He leaned forward, capturing my eyes with his once again. His eyes lit with alpha will.

The asshole was going to try to command me. I released part of my wolf, heading him off.

"Well, what do we have here?" Liam slipped into the booth next to me and wrapped an arm around my shoulders. He leaned forward, cutting off his dad's challenge. "You wouldn't be trying to command my mate to leave now, would you?"

"Well, you won't listen." His dad leaned back in the seat.

Why hasn't he tried doing that to you? If he'd commanded Liam, then we wouldn't even need to be here having this discussion.

He did. Liam's arm tensed around me. *Why did you think I disappeared for all those weeks? He let me go to the game, because hell, I'm the quarterback. Then when I saw you again, it all went out the window. Our bond is stronger than his will.* "So, you've resorted to bribing her?"

"This is career suicide." His dad glanced around and then released a low growl. "You're going to ruin the very thing you've been training for your entire life."

"By mating with me?" It was all bullshit and just a way for him to control Liam. "He's still the same person. How do I taint him?"

"Because fated mates make us weak." He pointed to me and shook his head in disgust. "It's okay for people like you to have their fated. It makes you feel like you have a meaning in life and are important to someone."

It was almost like listening to someone from a different planet speak. For someone to be representing our people, he sure didn't have a good impression of them.

"A council member doesn't need that kind of bullshit." His dad took in a deep breath and took another sip of his coffee.

Has he always been like this? It was hard to believe that someone like this man had such caring and loving children.

Oh, wait. It gets better. Liam snickered in our bond.

"We are important to not just one person but to everyone." He lifted his head high and straightened his shoulders. "It's our duty to reject our fated mate because all they can do is make us lose our focus or worse."

Should we tell him who I am? Maybe if he knew I was the overseer, he'd stop giving us a hard time about being together.

Hell, no! Liam's fingertips brushed my arm. *We can't tell a single soul, not until the time is right.*

So when is that going to be? I kind of wanted to know what he considered as the appropriate time.

When we find out what happened to your father or we're strong enough to not bend to the council's will. We can't risk telling them and putting you in danger.

But he's your dad. I figured he would have jumped at the opportunity. It might make his dad lay off him.

Exactly. He scooted closer to me, our legs brushing. *But for the first time, something doesn't feel right with him. I can't risk you just to make my life easier.*

"You said, the last time we met here with Bree, that I had a strong wolf." I had to use his own words against him. "So now you aren't okay with that?"

"I meant at a city or district alpha level." He pointed to his son. "Not to this level. You weren't even raised to see how things are supposed to be done. This is something you're born into. You can't just fall into it."

"Well, she has." Liam dropped his arm and stood. "And it's final. She's not going anywhere."

"I could easily pull her scholarship." He grinned as he threatened me.

"And I could easily go to another college." Liam took my hand and tugged me toward him. "If you want to play with fire, I can do it too. I understand that you don't agree with my decision, but frankly, I don't give a flying fuck. Where she goes is where I'll be."

We had to put an end to this argument now. "And there's no amount of money that will make me leave him. I'm not with him for power or whatever the hell you might think it is. I love him. If he chooses to walk away from it all, I'll be right there beside him."

Mr. Hale's body was so tense I doubted he could breathe. His eyes were full of anger, and he knew he had been backed into a corner. He needed Liam or everything would go to hell for the council.

"I hope you two know what you're doing." He stood and threw a fifty dollar bill on the table and placed his checkbook in his suit pocket. "Both of you are playing a very dangerous game. One for which you obviously don't understand the ramifications."

"Are you threatening us?" Liam's eyes darkened.

"No, of course not, but I don't think either of you is thinking everything through." He shook his head as he clenched his jaw.

"It's a done deal." Liam tugged my hand as we took the first step away. "Instead of trying to figure out a way to get us to break apart, why don't you try being supportive and find a way to make it easier for us to be together? There is absolutely nothing left for us to discuss."

The two of us headed to the door, and I turned around to see Mr. Hale's hate-filled eyes locked straight on me.

He made us play our hand, and Liam stole the control from him. I'd hoped the conversation could've gone smoother, but there was no reasoning with his father, at least for now. I only hoped we could at some point soon.

CHAPTER FOUR

When we made it back to the dorm, Liam pulled me into his arms. "I'm so damn sorry."

"What's wrong?" Bree popped her head out of the kitchen, which only had a small wall separating it from the den.

"Dad tried to buy her off." Liam's voice was low, filled with anger.

"What do you mean buy her off?" She entered the den and glanced at me.

"He placed a checkbook on the table and asked me what it would take to get me to leave." I still couldn't get over that. What kind of parent did that?

"Oh my God." Her eyes widened. "He's been acting strange here lately, but I didn't expect that."

"Not only that, but I entered the restaurant to find him trying to use his alpha will to make her leave." He kissed my forehead and took a deep breath. "Thank God you're stronger than that."

"Wait." Bree's brows furrowed. "How the hell is that possible?"

We need to tell her. I hated keeping the secret from her. She was my best friend and my ally even after how the whole Kai thing had gone down. *She deserves to know.*

Fine. Liam stepped back, giving me the opportunity. *But only her.*

I turned to face her, almost afraid of her reaction.

If I thought she'd be angry, *I'd tell you.* Liam took my hand and turned to face his sister as well. *The longer you wait, the more upset she'll be.*

"Tell me what's wrong instead of mind speaking to one another." Bree's voice was a little louder than normal, and her heart was picking up speed.

"So... other than Liam and me completing our bond this weekend and Max getting hurt, there was something else that happened." I was making it sound so ominous, and in a way, it kind of was.

"Okay..." She bit her bottom lip and bounced on her feet.

"I found out that my father isn't my biological father." I took a deep breath as Liam squeezed my hand. "My blood father was named Brent Forrest."

"What?" Bree's mouth dropped open, and she stumbled a step back. "As in the overseer who died? But Dad and the other members said he didn't have an heir." Her eyes went straight to Liam.

"Because my mom had just found out she was pregnant before he left to meet with the council." Maybe it wasn't a good idea to tell her. Her face was a shade paler, and she was blinking repeatedly like she didn't quite comprehend what she'd heard. "And he told her if he didn't make it back, then she was to run and hide ... to protect me."

"Wait..." She lifted a hand in the air and took a deep

breath. "Are you insinuating the council had something to do with this?"

"Yes, I am." If I was going to tell her that my dad was the overseer, might as well include the whole truth. "He was going to expose them for something, and they made sure it didn't happen."

"Do you hear what she's saying?" Bree focused on her brother again. "I mean, Dad is no saint, but he wouldn't be up for hurting his best friend. Her mom must have lied."

"I was there. She was telling the truth." Liam took a step in front of me. "I didn't like hearing it either. Honestly, I wasn't super thrilled with us telling you this, but Mia wanted to. This isn't about you, so pull your head out of your ass."

There was a moment of silence before Bree burst out laughing.

Uh... is she okay? She went from hurt and upset to laughter within seconds.

Yeah, it's her creepy-ass way of handling difficult information. Liam shook his head and tugged me over to the couch beside him.

"I can't believe this." Bree shook her head and took in a deep breath. "Maybe Nate isn't all that crazy after all."

Liam placed his arm on the back of the chair, around my shoulders. "What does that mean?"

"He said that the council had changed, especially in the last year or so." Bree sat in the recliner and wiped away a tear that had rolled down her cheek from her laughing fit. "More and more, people are unhappy with how they are being led. Their hardships and needs are being ignored."

"And that's why you don't need to be around him," Liam growled deep in his chest.

I turned around and smacked him hard. "You don't get to say shit like that."

"Uh, yes, I do." He nodded toward Bree. "She's my sister and kind of has to listen to me."

"First off, you're her brother, not her father." I held up two fingers. "And secondly, how did you like it when people were trying to break us apart?" I arched an eyebrow.

"But, what they don't know is you're the overseer." He smirked as if he thought he'd won the argument.

"When you claimed me, you had no clue I was the overseer." I leaned over and kissed his cheek. "But it's cute that you tried winning."

He frowned.

"I'm so glad to have you here in our life." Bree's smile lit up her entire face. "Maybe, for once, I can spend more time with Nate."

"But he knows about the rebellion." Liam's brow furrowed. "That can't be good."

"Nate's a great guy. He's my brother's best friend." My phone began buzzing in my pocket, and I pulled it out. "Speak of the devil." Max's name appeared on caller ID. "Let me take this."

I stood and headed to my bedroom. He still hadn't gone back to school yet after what had happened Sunday. We dropped him off at our parents' house, and they told him everything they'd told me. I wanted to stay, but considering what was going on back at the academy, we weren't able to stay long. "Hello?"

"Hey." Max's strong voice filled the line. "How are you doing?"

"I'm okay. Are you healed up yet?" We'd only texted since the news dropped, making our conversation seem a little off.

"Yeah, I'm heading back to school now. Coach has been blowing my phone up, but I needed time to process everything." He took in a deep breath. "You know that you're my sister, and it doesn't change things between us, right?"

It hurt that his tone was so unsure. He should know me better than that. "You're my brother, and your father is still my dad. This changes absolutely nothing. You are still the boy who'd bring me chicken noodle soup when I felt bad." He and his dad had been there in all the ways that mattered and counted as family. "You're still the same guy who would sneak out and shift, running to our favorite spot to talk. I love you, and nothing has to change ... unless you want it to."

"No, I'm so glad to hear you say that." He chuckled. "I know Mom and Dad said that's how you had reacted, and we talked via text, but I needed to hear you say it out loud. I wanted to hear it without our parents' prying ears around."

That I understood all too well. "Maybe we can see each other one weekend. Hell, maybe this weekend, but let me check with Liam."

"You can't go anywhere without his permission now?" His tone was a little deeper as if he didn't approve of it.

"No, but he has a football game I need to be at too. Maybe we could meet up Sunday, and I'll bring Bree along so she can see Nate." That sounded like fun and a good opportunity to get Liam to warm up to Nate.

"You're going to bring Liam with Bree and expect Nate to be around too?" He didn't sound convinced.

"Yup. You'll see." I'd always enjoyed a good challenge. "Let's plan on it."

"Sounds good to me." He chuckled. "If anyone can make it work, it's you."

Liam walked into my bedroom and headed straight to

me, pulling me into his arms. "Okay, I'll see you this weekend, I've got to go."

"All right, I love you." He hung up the phone.

And at that moment, everything felt like it might work out.

I HURRIED over to the football stadium bright and early Thursday morning. Evan had told me to wear something comfortable for sparring, a change of clothes, and to wear my hair up. I found it oddly specific that he even went as far as to address my hair.

Liam had tried going with me despite Evan's insistence for him to stay away, so it was fun leaving the dorm without him. I'd bet he was still standing at the door scowling. He didn't like to lose. However, when I pointed out it was for me to learn how to fight and defend myself, which couldn't be done with him growling every time Evan got near me, he conceded.

He made me promise to make it up to him for all the emotional turmoil it would put him through this morning. I had a very good idea about what kind of compensation he wanted, and my body warmed at the idea.

When I reached the doors Bree and Kai had taken us through at the football game, I paused. There wasn't a guard outside, so I wasn't quite sure how I'd get in.

"You didn't take my advice." A deep voice came from behind, startling me.

I spun around and came face to face with the football coach.

He narrowed his honey eyes as he adjusted his Wolf Moon ball cap on his head. He was wearing the standard blood-red jersey with Wolf Moon written in silver, and black shorts. He had to be in his forties but looked like a man in that age range, unlike the youthful-looking council members.

"What advice was that?" He scared the crap out of me, so my mind wasn't functioning right yet.

"To stay away from them." He shook his head and blew out a breath. "But according to what I've heard, instead, you've wrapped yourself more into them than even I am. Good luck with that." He reached around me, using his badge to unlock the door. "Let's go. He's already in there."

He held the door open for me, and I passed through, still reeling from that odd conversation. Why would he say that to me if he thought I was so entwined with them? Wouldn't he be afraid that I would tell Liam?

When we reached the split, instead of going left as we had for the game, he took a right, heading down to the door on the left.

"Wait, isn't that the men's locker room?" There were some things I'd rather leave to the imagination.

"Yeah, but you walk into the football team's private gym first." He grinned at me. "Afraid you might see something you like or don't like?"

Okay, this guy officially gave me the creeps. "Uh... I don't think Liam would take me seeing anything all that well." That was the best thing I could come up with at the moment.

"Oh, yes. Your mate." He headed down the hallway and opened the gym door for me. "After you, princess."

I hurried into the gym and almost sighed with relief when my huge-ass trainer came into view.

He was lifting some free-standing weights. It looked like

he was lifting three-hundred pounds without breaking a sweat or straining at all.

This room didn't have any machines. It was full of weights and a huge mat for only God knew what.

Evan turned to me and nodded. "Good. You listened."

"You may want to warn her about being aware of her surroundings." The Coach headed toward a desk in the back of the room. "I caught her by surprise; and I wasn't being quiet at all."

"Yeah, she's got a lot to learn." He shook his head and sighed. "Is your shoulder healed?"

"Yeah, it's fine." I had finally healed by Wednesday morning. Thank God for quick healing shifter genes.

"All right." He pointed to the mat. "At least Kai had you build up some strength, so that should bode well for you. Let's begin with some basic stances. Coach, I'll need your help."

"Okay." He put down his drink and headed over. "What do you need?"

"Grab one of the punching bags." He pointed to a bag laying against the wall.

"Got it." He walked over and picked it up.

"Why is he here?" It struck me as odd, and I couldn't get past it.

"Well, one ... Technically, it's his gym, but the main reason is that he's the only one who can fight against me if I need to do a demonstration." He shrugged as the coach carried the bag over to us.

The coach placed the bag in front of us. "There you go."

"All right. So, watch me." He got into a fighting stance where his hands were in front of his face.

"Wait. Don't we need boxing gloves?" I glanced around, expecting to find some.

"We're wolf shifters, not pussies. Come on." He pivoted on his toes and punched the bag, making it fall into the coach.

The coach pushed it back upright.

Okay, so he was here as his helper. That was kind of interesting.

"Now, it's your turn." He waved his hands in front of his face. "Get in a fighting stance, and pivot with your right foot as you swing your punch outward. Remember to lead with your elbow."

It all seemed to run together, but I did the best I could. As I punched the bag, it barely moved. "What the hell?" I'd expected at least a small swing or something. It was like I didn't hit the damn thing.

The corners of Evan's lips tilted upward, or at least, I thought they did. His expression was always a mask of indifference. "It just means we have a lot more to make up for than I realized. Again."

I wasn't sure how long I kept hitting the damn thing, but it felt like days at this point. My arms were like gelatin, and the only thing I worked on today was punching the damn bag. He did have me rotate between my left and right side, which I wasn't sure if it was better or worse.

"You have to make it tilt on the edge before you can leave today." Evan met my eyes, challenging me.

Even though I'd never taken kickboxing before, I knew humans could move the damn thing. Why the hell couldn't I? I lifted my arms back up, ready to take the damn thing down. I didn't care if I had to go all Tarzan, straddling it to make it go down. I wasn't sure how much more of this I could take, and technically he didn't tell me it had to be with my arms.

I took a deep breath and steadied myself. I pulled deep down within and connected with my wolf. She purred in response. As I struck out, I pivoted on the bottom of my foot and led with my elbow. When my fist connected with the bag, it fell over to the ground. What the hell?

"Hot damn." A proud smile filled Evan's face. "You did it."

The coach shook his head and grabbed it, lifting it to stand it up. "How the hell did she do that? She had almost the same force as you."

"She channeled her wolf." His smile didn't falter when he stared into my eyes. "Your wolf is way stronger than I gave her credit for. Good job. You're done for the day."

He was breathtaking when he smiled. Not that I wanted to act on it, but I hadn't realized just how handsome he actually was until now. "That's it?"

"Yup, you channeled your wolf to knock the bag down." He nodded his head.

"Wait. Why didn't you tell me to do that in the first place? And how can a human knock down something like that when it took me all day."

"You didn't tell her this was made specifically for a gym full of wolf shifter football players?" The coach smirked and shook his head. "Damn."

"She didn't need to know. She had to get frustrated in order to figure the rest out." He reached over and patted my arm. "Besides, you need to learn how to fight with your wolf, and you needed to figure it out on your own. Now go on and get out of here. You'll want to take a hot shower; you'll be hurting in the morning."

I wasn't sure what else to say, but the information hit me

to the core. I'd grown up around more humans than wolves, so I never had to fight someone stronger or bigger than me. It took being here before I figured it out.

As I walked out the door, I heard the coach mumble to Evan. "She shouldn't be that strong. That's damn near impossible unless she was one of the elite alphas."

I shut the door as I tapped into my wolf. I could barely make out Evan's response.

"Yeah, something doesn't seem right, but I'll get to the bottom of it."

Maybe having Evan train me was a bad idea. He could figure out my secret. I had to go talk to Liam now.

CHAPTER FIVE

My body felt like it was numb—that's how damn sore I was, and I hadn't even made it halfway back to the dorm. Maybe Kai was right; I could've used a couple more months of weight training.

As I approached the dorm, I heard some voices that made me pause.

"You know it makes more sense for him to be with me, not *her*." Amber's overly entitled voice filled my ears.

"No, no I don't." Bree's voice was stiff and unyielding. "She cares for him."

"Oh, that's bullshit, and you know it." Amber's voice was fierce.

I stepped into the trees, moving slowly until I was able to see both women through a hole made by some branches. I was still a good fifty feet away.

"No, it's not." Bree's pink face made her blue eyes stand out more. "Unlike you, she doesn't give a damn about his position or that one day he'll be powerful. She's genuine and cares not only about him but me too."

"How has she been able to manipulate the two of you?"

Amber threw her hands in the air. "Maybe I could expect it from you, but not Liam. He's always been able to call people out on their shit."

"Someone sounds jealous." Bree stood tall and, for once, let her strong wolf shine through. "You do realize there are three other heirs you could try to..." She huffed and rolled her eyes, "negotiate with."

"It is business." Amber scoffed and clenched her hands into fists. "If you start letting your heart rule, then you're weak ... a nothing."

Dear God. Had they all been raised this way? It was so foreign to me after what my parents had instilled in me.

"No. I think we've all become weak because we've removed the heart from the process." Bree shook her head and narrowed her eyes. "Something that Liam and I are starting to realize with Mia in our lives. So instead of fighting it, accept it. She's part of our family now and won't be going anywhere."

"Your dad isn't sold on that." Amber flipped her long hair over her shoulder. "So, it'll be victorious when I see both of you fall."

"Dad doesn't have any say in it." She took a step toward the girl, her eyes glowing. "Liam and I are both willing to walk away from it all."

"Liam would never..." The words left her mouth, but she paused.

She didn't even believe what she was saying.

"Try him." Bree smirked. "I dare you."

"This isn't over." Amber turned on her heel and headed toward the building across the field.

If I'd had any doubts about Bree's loyalty, they were gone now. I stepped from the trees and hurried over to her.

When I turned the corner, Bree's eyes fell on me and she sighed. "I guess you heard everything."

"Yeah, are you okay?" I hated that they both were going through so much, all because of me. I never meant for any of this to happen, but at the same time, maybe they needed everything shaken up in order to remember what was really important.

"I'm fine." She snorted and raised her eyebrows. "I've always hated that bitch, and she made Liam even more of an asshole than he already was."

"Well, we don't need that." I couldn't imagine a grouchier Liam. Granted, the past few days, he appeared to be mellowing out ever so slightly.

"We definitely do not." She snorted as she glanced over at me. "You look like shit. What did Evan do to you?"

"It was rough, but he did more for me in one session than Kai had in the past month and a half." I hadn't realized how true that was until I said the words. In one training session, I went from barely making the bag move to almost kicking its ass like Evan did.

"That's a good thing, right?" She glanced at her phone and sighed. "I've got to go or I'm going to be late. I'll catch up with you after class."

"Yeah, I'll see you later." I stood there and watched her hurry off to her class.

Right when I was about to head into the dorm, I saw Amber run off out of the corner of my eye. She was heading toward the stadium.

What could she be doing? It couldn't be anything good. Was she going to try to hit on Evan or something? Someone needed to put that bitch in her place.

I followed behind her, keeping close to the woods.

She glanced around as if she could feel herself being

stalked, but she didn't slow her speed. In fact, she increased it.

I had to be careful; there was no telling what she would do if she caught me. I had a gut feeling she was up to something important, but I had no clue what the hell it could be.

When she broke into the clearing, something snapped right beside me in the woods. As I turned to see who was sneaking up on me, a hand with some sort of handkerchief went over my nose. Before I could jerk away, my head began to swim. Shit. *Liam, I need help.*

Where are you? His words were full of anxiety.

But before I could respond, darkness overcame me.

I woke with a startle. My neck ached as I lifted it, and all I could see was black. There was something over my eyes, keeping me blindfolded. I tried moving my arms, but they were restrained on what felt like armrests. What the hell? *Liam?*

Oh, thank God. Liam's voice was rough and pained. *Where the hell are you?*

I... I don't know. I shifted in my seat, but my legs couldn't move. Chains rattled as my feet were stuck in place. *I'm blindfolded and chained to a chair, I think.*

Is there anything you can make out? Liam's fear was clear through the bond.

Or at least, I thought it was his. Hell, it could have been mine for all I knew. *No, nothing. Other than a dingy musk.*

"She's awake." A guy's voice I'd never heard before came from right behind me. "What... What do we do?"

"Knock her ass back out." I heard another man's voice, and then someone's feet scuffed the ground.

They're about to knock me out again. I didn't know what the hell to do. I couldn't fight or run. I was helpless. I'd never felt so weak before in my entire life. I didn't like it, and to be honest, I was scared shitless.

I'm going to find you; just hold on. I'll be there soon. We have a lead. His voice was a deep growl even through the mind link.

Someone was now over my shoulder, I heard them moving as a hand moved from behind me and around to my face. "I'm sorry, but we have no choice."

My head grew light as the cloth pressed against my nose again. *I love you.* I needed him to know that, in case I never got a chance to talk to him again.

I love you too. He sounded broken as blackness engulfed me once more.

A FAINT GROWL stirred me from my sleep this time. I tried moving, ready to fight whomever was close by, but again, I couldn't move. That's when everything sank back in. I was blindfolded and chained to a chair. *Liam?*

We're here. Liam linked back with me. *We're coming for you.*

My heart began to race. I had no clue where I was, who was around me, or anything. I tried to calm my racing nerves and focus.

"Shit, what do we do?" The anxiety-ridden man from earlier was pacing in front of me. "He told me to stay back here and make sure nothing happens, but if it's them, we're dead."

Them? I wanted to ask the question, but I was afraid he'd stop speaking. I tried not to move despite my neck screaming in pain. I needed to lift it, but then he'd know I was awake.

A howl echoed against the walls.

"Dammit." The guy shuffled his way over to me and leaned close to my ear. "Wake up. We've got to move."

Oh, hell no. I wasn't going anywhere. I stayed perfectly still, making sure my breathing stayed even.

"What the fuck am I supposed to do?" His heart started racing, and he began jerking on my arm. "I can't push the chair out of here. I guess I'll have to carry her."

I considered that this could be my chance. I tried to remain limp so he wouldn't catch on.

He shuffled and sounded like he might be digging something out of his pockets. "She's light. It shouldn't be a problem." He bent down and began rattling the chains. "There we go."

There was a click down at my left ankle. I had to take deep calming breaths so my heart rate didn't skyrocket and alert him to me being conscious.

Footsteps pounded outside, heading toward us.

"Shit." The guy mumbled as he fumbled with what had to be the key. He grabbed the key again right as something pounded against the door. "No." The guy grabbed the other chains, rattling them.

Another loud bang hit the door.

"Let us in or you're going to regret it." Micah's deep voice came from behind the door.

The guy managed to unlock the other leg, but before he had a chance to remove the key, I kicked my left leg straight out as hard as I could.

"Ow!" The guy yelled as he stumbled backward.

"Mia?" Micah yelled again as something pounded on the door once more, causing a loud cracking sound.

I tried to open my mouth to yell back, but there was a large piece of tape over it. Dammit, I hadn't even noticed that until now.

"Dammit, we've gotta go." The guy sounded like he'd gotten back on his feet. "Where is the inhalant?"

Something rammed against the door again, and I heard another loud crack.

"No." The guy's voice sounded scared and shaky.

The door opened, and the musky scent of a shifter in wolf form filled my nose.

"Look, I, uh, didn't have a choice," the guy stammered.

The wolf growled, and I heard its paw hit the ground fast.

A hand touched me, and I jerked back.

"It's just me." Micah's voice was right next to my ear, and then he touched me again on my arm. "I'm going to take this blindfold off you."

I was glad for the warning because when he removed it, the light hurt my eyes. I blinked several times as he bent down, getting the key out of the lock. After a few seconds, my eyes adjusted to my surroundings, and I turned to find a familiar shaggy blond wolf charging an older man who seemed to be barely holding his own. Although I hadn't seen him since the tour, I'd recognize Kai anywhere.

I glanced around, taking in where the hell I was. It looked like an old automobile repair shop. There were empty cabinets shoved against the walls, and a small, portable table with three chairs sat in the corner about twenty feet away from me. The ground was concrete, and dust coated everything. Where the garage doors should have been was replaced with steel doors. I glanced across the area to the single door that opened into the room.

"Liam is about to go out of his mind." Micah shook his head as he unlocked my left hand.

Micah's found me. As he unlocked my other hand, I grabbed the end of the tape and grimaced. This was going to hurt. I took a deep breath and ripped it from my lips. Damn, that hurt.

I'll be there soon. Liam's words were a promise.

"Do you know how much trouble you're causing us?" Micah's golden eyes were full of annoyance and seemed even lighter against his dark olive skin. His athletic frame was stiff, and his black shirt molded to his muscles. The southern heir was only a few inches taller than me, but he was filled with disdain. "If it wasn't for Liam losing his damn mind, none of us would be here."

"Thanks for your concern." Even though Micah was an asshole, he was nothing compared to Simon.

I turned my focus over to Kai's wolf form, who was forcing the older man into a corner.

The older man lifted both hands in the air. "Look, I'm not even shifting. I don't mean any harm."

"Says the guy who kidnapped me." Was he really trying to act like the victim right now?

"Look, it wasn't anything personal." The older man stumbled back as Kai continued to circle him. "We needed payment, but I still can't figure out why they're here." He pointed to Micah.

I spun around. "Did you hire them?"

"What? No." Micah's eyes widened. "Even if I don't like you and wish you would go away, I wouldn't do that. Not to Liam. He's too unstable about you right now."

Something sounded from the back. When I turned around, I saw another wolf enter the room. It wasn't someone I recognized.

"Micah, who is that?" I pointed to the door.

He spun around, and his whole body tensed. "I don't know." He shook his head. "Stay back. You can't fight in your condition."

Micah shifted right in front of my eyes, his clothes shredding. He bared his teeth at the wolf, who didn't appear impressed.

I wasn't sure what the hell to do. I wasn't a helpless damsel in distress, but at the same time, I didn't want to cause more problems. The heirs hated me enough already.

Micah's dark brown wolf charged at the other and went straight for the jugular. At the last second, the tan wolf rolled to the right and got back on its four legs.

I turned to find the man, who had appeared to be helpless, holding a gun. His hands shook as he held it directly at Kai, which made the man even more dangerous. A scared gun wielder did stupid things.

There was no way I could stay on the sidelines while both of them risked their lives for me. *Liam, are you okay?*

Yes, I'm almost there. He howled, and it didn't sound far away at all.

At least, he was near.

The tan wolf attacked Micah. He raised up on his two hind legs and landed on Micah's back. Micah immediately fell backward, throwing all of his weight so that he landed hard on the other wolf.

Kai bared his teeth at the scared man and ran straight at him. Kai's eyes locked on the hand holding the gun.

Micah stood back up on his four legs, and he went for the wolf's neck. The other wolf countered his move, moving his neck, but it was too little too late. Micah sunk his teeth into his flesh, causing the other wolf to wail.

When the older man turned around to find out what

was happening, his eyes widened as he saw his friend being taken out. Kai was only inches from his hand when the guy aimed his gun at Micah at the last second.

No.

The gun went off, and I jumped in front of Micah. Even though he didn't like me, he had just saved me, and I couldn't let him go like that.

Mia! No! Liam's dark brown wolf ran into the room a split second before the bullet hit me in my left shoulder. The impact forced me to fall backward, and I thudded to the ground.

CHAPTER SIX

R aw pain poured through me. When the bullet had first hit, I hadn't felt anything, but now it was the most excruciating pain I'd ever experienced.

Liam's dark brown wolf ran to me, his frightened eyes looking me over.

I'm fine. Obviously, I wasn't, but the truth wasn't going to put him in the right headspace.

Don't even lie to me right now. His wolf whimpered as he sniffed my wound.

Evan ran into the room in human form, his eyes landing on me. He hurried over, dropping down beside me. "Mia, what the hell happened?"

"The man that Kai is fighting." I stopped, taking a deep breath. The pain seemed worse when I spoke. "Tried to shoot Micah." I turned my head to find Micah staring at me with blood dripping from his mouth. The man he'd been attacking lay still at his feet.

Then, I turned my head to Kai. He had the guy's hand that had been holding the gun crushed between his teeth, not letting him get free. The gun was only a few feet away from them.

Thank God, neither one of them was hurt, or I'd have gotten shot for no good reason.

Evan squatted down beside me and gingerly touched my shoulder.

A deep growl emanated from Liam.

"Stop it." Evan glared at him. "I'm checking her wound. You're being an idiot." He placed his hand on my shoulder. "I need you to sit up so I can see whether it went all the way through your body."

"Okay." I wanted to say no, but there was no point. We had to see how bad off I really was. I gritted my teeth as I began to rise. The pain was so bad I felt dizzy, but I pushed through it. Luckily, Evan helped me up with my good shoulder.

"It didn't go through." He took a deep breath. " It's not lethal, but we'll need to get the bullet out as soon as possible before she bleeds out." His eyes went to Liam. "Go round the others up. We need to figure out who took her and why so we can leave and get her cleaned up."

Liam shook his head no. *I'm not leaving you.*

Please, I want to go home. I stared into his eyes, desperate.

Fine. He backed away and ran out the door. *Call me if it gets worse. This will only take a few minutes.*

"I can't believe you took a fucking bullet ... for him." Evan's gaze flickered at Micah and then settled back on me. "He's been an asshole to you."

"In all fairness, haven't all four of you been?" It was meant to be a joke, but it fell flat.

Evan winced at my words. "Yes. Yes, we have." He stood up on his feet again and glanced at me. "Can you stand?"

"I think... so." God, it really hurt, but it wasn't like being on my feet was going to make it any worse. Warm blood spilled down my shirt and onto the ground. "Why are you in human form?"

"The same reason Micah was supposed to be. All of us heirs aren't in the same pack, so we can't communicate in wolf form. Some of us must stay human. Micah and I are the strongest in human form, so it makes sense that we stand on two legs instead of four. We have a change of clothes in the SUV just in case something like this happens though. We all need to be in human form to handle this." Evan flattened his hand and pushed hard on my wound.

A loud groan left me, and my head began to spin. "Aw, shit. A little warning would've been nice." Tears spilled out of my eyes, and I had to remind myself to breathe.

Micah's dark brown wolf moved to stand behind me, supporting some of my weight. A small whimper left him.

It was strange having two heirs take care of me. If this would've happened just two weeks ago, they all would've left me behind to die.

"I promise I'll behave." The older man's voice shook, and for the first time, I got a good look at him.

He was balding and on the thinner side. He had to be around the same height as me, but there was something truly odd about him. His eyes looked younger than his actual appearance. He tried to lift both of his too-thin hands in the air and then took a deep breath.

Kai growled but dropped the man's hand from his mouth. He ran over and grabbed the gun before trotting back over to us.

"Look, I'm sorry. I didn't mean for any of this to happen." The man grabbed his wrist and held on to it tight.

Right then, a sandy brown wolf entered the room,

walking backward as he growled and stared right at the tall man stepping through the door. Liam came from behind as they herded the other man next to the scared one.

"We've got it from here." Evan nodded at them. "You have to put pressure on your wound. I need to keep an eye on these two idiots while the others shift back."

I'll be back in a moment. Tell Micah and Simon to stay while Kai and I shift back. Liam nodded at Kai, and the two headed for the door.

"Micah and Simon, Liam wants you to stay here and be back up for Evan until they get back here."

Simon growled but went to sit next to Evan's feet as they stared the two men down.

"I told you this was a stupid idea." The older man shook his head. "This was bound to happen. When you get a task like that, you should know better than to say yes."

"Shut up." The other man growled.

The two men favored each other, but the more confident one seemed to be several years younger.

"I told you to listen to your father, but do you?" The older man shook his head as he stared right into my eyes. "When I saw her, I knew something wasn't right. She's different, and they're scared."

"I said shut up, Dad." The guy's eyes glowed with alpha will.

Evan walked over to them and arched an eyebrow. "Your dad may be on to something. I'd speak up if I were you."

"He's already said too much." He glared at his father.

Simon growled and headed toward them, taunting them.

The younger man stood still and huffed. "'This is ridiculous. You are just kids. Are you really expecting us to be scared?"

"We aren't the ones who are backed into a corner." Evan raised his eyebrow, and the corners of his mouth tipped slightly upward.

If I hadn't gotten to know him better, I wouldn't have even noticed it. When I first met him, I'd thought he was expressionless, but he wasn't. It was just that varying emotions caused only slight changes to his overall indifferent features.

Liam breezed back into the room in human form with Kai right on his heels.

"We've got to get her medical help." Liam came over to me, his eyes on my face. *I can feel the pain you're in.*

"I can take care of it." Evan turned toward his friend. "We just need to get back on campus. It's not lethal, but I bet it hurts like hell."

"Are you sure?" Liam looked at my blood-soaked clothes and the puddle of blood that was growing beneath me.

"Yes, but the sooner the better." Evan arched an eyebrow.

"Simon and Micah, go shift back." Liam's eyes landed on the two men in front of us and the unconscious wolf on the floor. "We've got to take care of business."

The two wolves nodded and ran out the door.

Liam touched my face and leaned his head toward mine, breathing me in.

Despite the pain, I relished his touch. It felt like it had been so long since I'd seen him.

"Kai, will you help her?" Liam turned and looked at my friend, who stood several feet away, watching it all.

To say I was shocked wouldn't even begin to describe how I was feeling. Liam was willingly allowing Kai to help me. It almost seemed like I'd woken up in an alternate reality.

"Of course." Kai had another shirt in his hands, which he ripped into two pieces. "Here, let's put this around you. It'll do better than your hands."

As Kai positioned the shirt rags, tying them around my shoulder to cover the open wound, Evan and Liam sprang into action.

"Why did you kidnap my mate?" Liam's words were low but clear.

"Your mate?" The son's mask of indifference slipped. "She's ... your mate?"

"I told you this was strange." The older man shook his head.

"You're not helping." The son glared at his father.

"I'm going to ask nicely one more time," Liam growled the words. "Why did you kidnap my mate?"

"We didn't know she was your mate." The son's face lost some of its confidence.

Evan reared back and punched the younger one square in the jaw, making him crumple to the ground.

"And you thought they'd protect us." The older man laughed. "They send us after one of their own heirs' mates. I told you to ask more questions."

My world seemed to tilt. One of the council members had sent them after me. Mr. Hale wasn't lying when he said he wanted me gone.

Kai tightened the torn shirt around my arm, making me groan in pain.

"Be easy with her." Liam glanced back and scowled at Kai.

"The tighter it is, the better it will staunch the blood

flow." Kai lifted both hands in the air and stepped back. He glanced at me. "I'm sorry."

"No, it's fine." I was losing a lot of blood, so anything that would cut down on it was good with me. My head was beginning to feel a little dizzy.

"Are you trying to say that one of our fathers paid you to do this?" Evan shook his head.

"Not just one; all of them." The old man shook his head, and his eyes landed on the wolf on the other side of the room. "I was their pack alpha, and I don't know what happened, but I can barely even shift anymore. They had to take charge, but their mother is struggling worse than me. We had bills to pay, so when the council called, we thought we might get a chance to get a healer to help her and me."

"Enough." Liam's chest heaved as Simon and Micah entered the room, dressed in jeans and black shirts. "Do you expect us to believe that?"

The room began to spin, and my legs gave out from underneath me.

Kai's strong hands wrapped around me. "She's losing too much blood."

"Simon. Micah." Liam glanced at them and then came over to me. "Deal with them the way you see fit."

"Hell, yeah." Simon's maniacal laugh echoed against the walls.

"Come on." Liam picked me up, cradling me in his arms.

My head landed on his chest, and the beating of his heart comforted me.

Why didn't you tell me you were getting dizzy? His face was lined with worry. "Evan, let's go. We have to go get her situated."

"Okay." Evan patted Micah on the back. "I'll be back to help clean this mess up."

You can't kill them. They were struggling. It didn't seem right, especially if it was for their own pack and family.

Honey, there's no way they can make it out of this alive. Liam headed to the door. *I can't be here to oversee it, and you won't last much longer if we don't get this bullet taken care of. The longer we wait, the more your wolf is going to try to heal over it, which won't be good. You could start bleeding internally.*

"Don't let her go to sleep." Evan caught up to Liam's side. "I'm going to get the car, but don't jar her." He rushed out the door ahead of us.

"I'm going to stay here." Kai touched my arm before frowning. "I'll check on you later."

Why in the world did you take that bullet? Liam moved slower, trying not to jar me.

Because it would've been a direct hit on Micah. The tall, dark, muscular man had saved me, and it didn't seem right for him to die. *I couldn't let that happen.*

We walked down a hallway, and the sound of a gunshot echoed in the halls.

"Please, I'm telling you the truth." The old man screamed.

"You tried killing one of our own," Simon shouted the words. "And blamed the council for your sorry-ass attempt."

"Calm down, Simon." Kai's voice was loud. "We aren't killing them. The council wants us to take these three to them."

Thank God. I took in a deep breath of Liam's comforting musky sandalwood scent. *I thought they'd kill them, and they don't deserve that.*

They don't deserve it? Liam shook his head, and his forehead creased. *They tried shooting Micah, and they kidnapped you. Because of them, you're bleeding.*

But you heard them. It was self-preservation. For some reason, it stopped me from hating them. They weren't doing it out of hate; they were protecting their pack. *It's sad that they had to resort to this in order to try to protect their pack and family.*

What do you mean? He hurried down the hallway, and some natural light soon filtered in.

I glanced around the room, trying to get my bearings. *Obviously, if they were in need like that, it'd been for years. Why didn't a city or district alpha step in? Isn't that their role? To tend to all the packs' needs and figure out how to help them?*

Yeah, it is. He furrowed his brows as we approached a glass double-door that had seen better days. There was a large crack in the glass of one door, and the other door was nothing but shattered shards littering the ground.

The bright sun bore down on us as we stepped outside.

I blinked several times until my eyes acclimated. There was no telling how long I had the blindfold on. The light didn't usually bother me like this.

The Escalade was pulled right up to the front, and the back door was open.

Evan was in the driver's seat and glanced over his shoulder. "Let's move."

Liam smoothly stepped into the backseat of the car and shut the door, cradling me in his arms. "Go."

Immediately, the car moved forward.

It was silent for a few moments before Evan glanced in the rearview mirror at Liam. "Do you think our parents really did this?"

"I don't know." Liam leaned his head down and pressed his lips to mine. *You've got to stay awake. You can't fall asleep. We're only ten minutes away from the academy.*

"Don't give me that bullshit." Evan's voice was his normal low scary one. "There was a reason I didn't make your ass leave her that night after the KSU football game. I wouldn't have trained her if I hated her. And damn, well, I like her. Besides, after seeing what she did for Micah, she's officially one of us to me. So, don't try to give me that half-assed answer. Don't hold back the truth."

My eyes began to close, and my heart warmed after hearing Evan's confession.

"Yeah, I think they did it." Liam touched my cheek. "Mia, keep your eyes open."

"Shit, we gotta get back there fast." Evan's voice was scared, and the car seemed to be moving faster. "Keep her awake."

"Mia." Liam took a hand and shook my face. "Stay with me."

I'm here. Even though I spoke the words in my mind, they even sounded slurred to me.

"Stay awake, please. Baby, please." Liam's voice cracked as he kissed my lips. "I need you to look at me."

It broke my heart to hear his words. I didn't want him to be upset with me, but there was less pain in the dark. I just needed to rest for a minute.

CHAPTER SEVEN

"Mia." Liam's voice entered my unconsciousness, urging me back to him.

It had hurt so bad; I didn't want to go back. It was kind of nice here in the darkness. I felt peace, which had been hard to find lately.

Something dug deep inside me, breaking through my protective barrier. I wanted to retreat further into the darkness. The pain, the hurt was so excruciating.

Mia, please wake up. His voice almost sounded like it was broken.

Though he was too strong for that. If Mom and Dad could move on from their fated, surely he'd be fine without me.

Another stabbing pain hit me, and my stomach roiled even here.

I need you. Please, open those beautiful green eyes. Through our bond, I felt his grief. *The bullet is out finally, but we need you to wake up.*

If I thought I knew what pain was, it was nothing compared to what he was feeling now. It felt as if a part of him was being ripped out. In a way, it was since I was the missing piece of his soul.

It was as if he was projecting into my mind; memories of our first kiss, our night of sex before he had disappeared, and then the day we claimed one another.

I don't know what I'd do if I lost you. I love you. His words were broken, and the pain of potentially losing me was taking over.

I couldn't hurt him like that. I needed to be with him. Why should the council be allowed to strip one more thing away from someone? Not only did I have my fated mate, who was desperate to stand beside me, but I had to find justice for my father. If not, then he had died in vain.

There was no way I was taking the easy way and backing out now. I took another second to enjoy the darkness, the peace, the once again pain-free space between, only God knew where. There was no bright, shining light or fire and brimstone. Was I stuck in some kind of purgatory?

Dammit, Mia. Wake up now. His voice had turned desperate. No longer was he begging; he was commanding.

I braced myself and opened my eyes to find both Liam and Evan hovering over me.

"Her eyes are open." Evan breathed out a sigh of relief as his face smoothed back into its normal features.

I glanced around a room that didn't look familiar. It had the standard silver of the school colors, but there was a huge-ass, blood-red leather couch that I was lying on. The pain hit me again, so hard that I almost felt like I couldn't breathe. *Where ... am I?* My stomach roiled as the pain somehow grew stronger.

You're in my and Evan's dorm room. Liam frowned as he glanced at Evan. "She's about to puke."

Now that he said the words, I realized that was exactly

what was about to happen. I moved to sit up, but even more pain washed over me. I had barely moved an inch.

Evan ran into the kitchen right as bile from my stomach began traveling up my throat. *I can't roll over.* I was going to puke all over myself. Dear God, this was going to get nasty.

Let me help. Liam leaned over and gently grabbed my shoulder. As he tried to help me turn to my uninjured side, I began dry heaving.

Evan slid a garbage can underneath me, and though I heaved, nothing but phlegm and bile came out.

"Shit, she's dehydrated." Evan's pale eyes deepened to a silver. "Did they not feed you or at least get you something to drink?"

Tears dripped down from my eyes as the last heave left my body. I sagged into the couch as Liam helped prop me up on my side. I tried to talk, but the pain seemed to take over, demanding deep breaths. *No, they didn't.*

"Are you fucking serious?" Liam's loud voice startled me, making my shoulder throb. "In the last three days, they didn't give you anything? Maybe we should take her to the hospital or something."

What? I'd been passed out for almost three days. It was a little crazy to believe. Every time I started to stir, they'd knocked my ass out again with some sort of inhalant sprayed into a handkerchief.

"You know we can't. She's a wolf, and it would make the humans suspicious. We both know our dads were behind this, so we can't take her to the infirmary either. We have to get her to drink water." Evan stepped back and raced into the kitchen. I heard several cabinet doors open and close. He sounded like he was getting some medicine out as he filled a glass with water. Within seconds, he was heading back in. "She needs to sip the water slowly and take a pain pill. If we don't get both of those into her, she's going to get a lot worse."

"But you said she needed to wake up," Liam's voice growled. "Why would we put her back to sleep?"

"Because if we couldn't, she would be in a world of trouble. But we were able to get her to regain consciousness." He held the pill out to me, but it hurt so damn much that I couldn't move my arm. "Take a few sips of water and sleep."

"She's in so damn much pain. I can feel it through our bond." Liam took the pill from his hands and placed it against my lips. "Here."

I opened my mouth, ready for anything to ease the pain.

"Are you sure it won't upset her stomach further?" Liam brushed his fingertips along my cheek. "She's already in so much pain."

"It'll be fine. It'll help her sleep." Evan patted his friend on the arm. "I promise I would never hurt her."

Liam stared into his friend's eyes, searching for something. He must have found whatever it was he needed because he held up the glass of water to me that Evan had blessedly put a straw in.

Not wasting another second, I took a sip of the cool, refreshing liquid and didn't want to stop. I was so thirsty, but I didn't realize how much until this moment. The pain couldn't even prevent me from taking three large sips.

"Hey, easy there." Liam pulled the straw from my mouth. "You can't get too much water in your empty stomach or you'll throw up everything, making this whole thing a lot nastier."

He was right, but dammit ... I was so thirsty, and the pain was all-encompassing.

"She needs some rest, and so do you." Evan stood and

turned off the lights. "I'm sure she'll call for you if she needs you."

"No, I'm staying right here." Liam sat on the ground next to me and laid his head down to touch mine.

"Okay." Evan went to the front door and opened it. "I'm going to go check on the others and see what they found out. I'll be back soon."

"See you." Liam's eyes stayed on me as he waved his friend off.

As soon as the door shut, Liam turned his head so he was looking into my eyes. "I'm so damn sorry, Mia. If my father had anything to do with this..."

We're here together now. I hated to see him hurt this much. It was close to being worse than my own physical pain.

"That's not the point." He took my hand and lightly caressed my fingers.

It was so gentle I could barely feel it, almost as if he thought touching me too hard would make it all worse. I was amazed by how much he had changed in such a short period of time. He was the caring mate that I, at one time, thought he'd never be. *I love you.*

I love you too. He sighed and chewed on his bottom lip. *Maybe by claiming you, I was being selfish. Look at what it's done to you.*

Don't ever say that. His guilt crashing into me like waves through our bond was suffocating. *This has all been worth it.*

Being kidnapped, shot, and dragged through the wringer has been worth it for you? He arched an eyebrow, and the concern on his face made him look like a broken man.

He wasn't though. *No, having my other half accept me and stand by me when I needed it means more to me than anything in this world. I wouldn't have it any other way.*

If it hadn't been for Kai, we wouldn't have found you. He sighed and leaned over, kissing me on the forehead. *Get some rest.*

My eyes grew heavy, and thankfully the medicine was taking the edge off, dissipating the pain. *What do you mean Kai found me?*

He somehow caught your scent and found you. Liam gave me a sad smile. *I guess I can't hate him much anymore. If it wasn't for him, there's no telling what would've happened to you.*

I told you he's a good friend. I took in a deep breath that made my shoulder scream at me. I couldn't stay awake much longer. I was so damn tired. *But he's not you.* For some reason, it felt like he needed to know that. *Ever since that party when I first laid eyes on* you, *it's always been you.* My eyes closed as my head began to fade into sleep.

This will never happen again. I promise you. His voice could have been a whisper of my mind, and his lips on my forehead could've been my imagination. Either way, I had never felt safer than with him by my side.

"THERE IS no way in hell I'm going to leave her." Liam's voice was only a whisper but stern.

My eyes began to flutter, and I found Mr. Hale standing at the door, talking to his son. His hair was slicked back, and he wore his usual black suit. His stance was confident but aloof. The only hint of his annoyance was the light flush that was evident in his cheeks. "Of course you will. This isn't an option. You will be taking your place on the council soon, and you need to visit some cities."

"Look at her." Liam's voice was rough. "She got shot. Did you find out who ordered those men to kidnap her?"

"No, absolutely not." His words were a little too hasty, and he averted his eyes to the ground as the faint smell of rotting eggs filled the air.

He was lying and acting guilty. That was the worst over-reaction I'd ever seen. Even toddlers could do better than that.

"You mean Simon, Micah, and the council weren't able to get any information from them?" Liam crossed his arms and arched his eyebrow. "I have a very hard time believing that, especially with Mr. Rafferty involved."

The one time I'd seen Evan's father was during a foot-ball game. It had been when Liam was fighting our bond and I'd gone there on a date with Kai. Liam was messing up left and right on the field because he was more focused on me than the game, so I snuck off to the bathroom. That was when I saw Mr. Rafferty physically attack Evan, demanding that he steal the spotlight from Liam while he was distracted. So, I had to agree with Liam. His dad would've beat the shit out of them to get any answers he wanted.

"Are you calling me a liar?" His dad's blue eyes iced over.

"Well, there is still time." Liam pointed at me. "She was clearly the target, and no one had learned about our rela-tionship yet, so you can't blame it on that."

"Who knows." Mr. Hale waved it off. "She's here obvi-ously, and they died before we could get clear answers."

"All three of them?" Liam's shocked voice spoke volumes. "That's a little extreme."

My breath suddenly felt like it was knocked out of me. Yes, those three people had kidnapped me, but they weren't malicious, and the older guy was nervous the whole time.

They were desperate to protect their family and friends, and now they were dead.

"As you suggested, Mr. Rafferty kept asking who hired them." Mr. Hale shrugged. "They kept insisting it was us, so he used more force. It wasn't our fault that they couldn't survive. They should've known better than to falsely accuse us, especially when we were the ones interrogating them."

"Yeah." Liam's voice was indifferent. It sounded similar to the cold Liam I'd known when we first met.

"Look, fall break is next week." His dad's eyes glowed as he tried forcing the alpha will on him. "You'll be going to visit several cities, starting Monday, with all the heirs. It'll give you time to feel better about her situation before you go."

"Okay." Liam nodded his head.

"Good." His dad blew out a breath he'd been holding in. "I had thought you'd be unreasonable and still fight me on this." He nodded his head, and I could feel his eyes land on me. "It's still not too late to change your mind."

"It's not happening." Liam's voice was deep, clear, and menacing. "If you mention it one more time, I won't be the well-behaved son you've always treasured."

"You know how I feel about threats." Mr. Hale narrowed his eyes at his son. "Just be ready to leave first thing Monday morning." He turned and headed out the door, slamming it behind him.

Liam turned around and met my eyes. "I'm sorry. Did he wake you?"

"No." I took a deep breath and winced, waiting for the mind-numbing pain. Only, it didn't come. It still hurt, but not like it had been. My body ached from lying on the couch on my side for so long, and I had to use the bathroom. "Do you think you could help me up?"

"Of course." He rushed over to me, holding me by my sides, and gently helped me sit up. "Are you sure you're up for this?"

I groaned as I sat, but once I got settled, it wasn't any worse than lying down. I glanced down at the couch and realized my blood coated it. It was hard to see since the couch was the same red color, but it was thick and a little darker. "I'm so sorry." I didn't mean to mess anything up.

"For what?" His eyes followed mine. "There is absolutely nothing for you to be sorry over. Dammit, Mia, you were shot."

"But that's a lot of blood." Damn, no wonder I had been so dizzy and out of it. "It might not come out."

"Then we buy a new couch." He sat next to me on the side without any blood and touched the top of my shoulder. "Can I see?"

He made it sound like buying a new couch wasn't a big deal. "Yeah, sure." I turned so he could see it.

As he moved my shirt, he had to cautiously peel it away from my skin. The blood had dried, causing the material to become stuck to my body.

"I think I need a shower." I felt gross and was hoping a shower might make me feel a little bit better. I was stiff all over. It had to be from sitting chained in that chair for days and then sleeping overnight on the couch.

"We need to be careful, but okay." He took my hand and led me to the hallway on the left of the couch. It wasn't long before we entered his room, which looked exactly like mine. The same bedding and everything. I sat on the bed, and his scent engulfed me.

He walked over to his closet and came out with a pair of my pajamas before heading straight to the shower to turn it on for me.

"How did you get those?" I asked as I pointed to the clothing and started moving ever so slowly into the huge marble bathroom.

"Evan snuck into your dorm and took a change of clothes for you." He put the clothes to the side of the large sink and grabbed two towels before stepping over to me. "Here, let me help you."

It didn't take long for him to help pull the clothes from my body, and I stepped into a warm shower, letting it wash over me. Liam followed a few seconds later, naked.

"What are you doing?" Despite my injury, my heart picked up its pace. He was so damn sexy, and how he'd been nursing me made my heart feel things that were well beyond the mate bond. At this point, even if he wasn't my mate, I'd have fallen in love with him anyway.

"Helping you get clean." He grabbed the bar of soap and stood close. "You aren't going to be able to move well."

He was right, and he was the only person I felt comfortable seeing me this fragile. My spirit had been stripped down, revealing how weak I was.

I kept my injured shoulder out of the direct spray. Honestly, even with Liam's help, it took a while for me to get clean, but soon I was stepping out.

Liam now focused on my body, and his eyes clouded over when he saw me. "You're so damn gorgeous." He reached down and picked up a clean white cotton wrap that was large enough to cover my bullet wound.

To be honest, the bullet wound itself wasn't that large, but damn, it hurt. He walked over and placed it, grabbing the gauze and tying it around my shoulder firmly. "I'm glad to see you're up and moving."

"Me too, but it's still painful. Is there a different pain pill

I can have?" It'd be nice to be able to drink some water and stay awake for a while.

He quickly got dressed. "Yeah, let me help you. Evan just got back." He helped me get dressed and even brushed my hair for me.

A few minutes later, we headed out to the kitchen and found Evan sitting at the table.

Evan already had a pain pill out and a glass of water with toast sitting next to it.

I grabbed the pill and drank some water, washing it down. My stomach was a little upset, but not like it had been. I picked up the piece of toast and took a bite. "Thank you."

"No problem." Evan gave me a smile that didn't meet his eyes. "You'll probably get sleepy soon, so plan on a nap or a lot of coffee."

"What's wrong?" Liam pulled out the seat at the round table and helped me get situated. "Did you find something out?"

"Yeah." Evan picked up his own glass of water and took a large sip. "So... apparently, those three didn't last very long."

"Dad said that they wouldn't cooperate and essentially your dad tortured them to death." Liam sat next to me and scooted his chair closer.

"Well, that was a nice way of putting it." Evan huffed and shook his head. "Kai and Micah informed me that as soon as they got back here to campus, they placed the three men in the basement room and left to go find the council. When they came back minutes later, the three men were already dead."

"You mean the council didn't question them after all." Liam stilled next to me.

"According to Kai and Micah, they weren't questioned. There wasn't enough time. They had been gone only five to ten minutes and never found the council." Evan ran a hand down his face. "The only logical explanation is that our dads were waiting in another room downstairs, and when Micah and Kai left to head to the council room to find them, they snuck in and killed them. Our dads had to have only wanted to bring them here to pretend to question them with the real intent of killing them on sight."

"But why?" None of this made any sense to me.

"Because the Council wanted to give the illusion that they tried even though they didn't." Liam took my hand in his. "This proves that they hired them."

The gravity of what he said took a second to fully sink in. The council had tried to hurt me, possibly even wanted me dead. If they had done that, what else were they capable of?

CHAPTER EIGHT

When Liam and I headed back to my dorm, we found Bree on the phone, pacing in a circle.

Her head snapped in our direction, and she cleared her throat. "She's here. I'll see you soon." There were dark circles under her eyes, and her body appeared to collapse as she blew out a huge breath.

"Are you okay?" Something bad must have happened.

"Am I okay?" Bree's voice was low at first but got higher. "Really?"

"Don't be a bitch, Bree." There was a warning in Liam's tone as he stepped in front of me. "She's only here because she insisted."

"What am I missing?" It was obvious she was very upset.

"My brother called your parents and me to ask if we knew where you might have gone off to." Bree pointed straight at her brother. "And then, I don't hear from him for three days and can't find you anywhere." She held up a hand. "Oh, wait. No, I found your cell phone in the corner of the woods where it had obviously been dropped."

"You didn't tell her you found me?" That didn't sound

right, especially if he made the time to call them in the first place.

I had just gotten off the phone with my parents, so I knew they'd been kept in the loop. Liam agreed to bring me home this weekend to see them. He didn't want to risk them coming on-site since his father was acting desperate. Max had already gotten hurt; we didn't need anyone else becoming easy prey.

"No, I didn't." Liam's eyes narrowed on his sister. "I knew she'd talk to Kai and he would let her know you'd been found."

"Had I known you were injured, I would've forced my way into his dorm." Bree's eyes were dark and filled with anger. "Kai mentioned to me this morning that you'd been shot and was wondering how you were doing. He asked if he could come by and visit you when Liam was here. So, of course, I called my brother to find out what the hell was going on. But I just kept getting his voicemail."

"Why didn't you tell her?" She had every right to be upset. Had the shoe been on the other foot, I'd have reacted the same way.

"Because she'd overreact like she is right now." Liam held his hand out, moving it up and down as he pointed his fingers in her direction. "You were hurt, injured, and needed rest."

"Had you told me that and let me peek in on her, I wouldn't be acting this way right now." Bree narrowed her eyes at him, and they took on a glow. "You still treat me like I'm a little kid that you have to keep in the dark."

"We had shit going on." Liam crossed his arms and looked down his nose at her. "Heir business."

"Stop it." I had to side with Bree on this one. "You should

have told her. How would you like it if the shoe was on the other foot? She's my family now, too."

"I thought I was doing the right thing." Liam glanced at me and sighed. "You're right." He focused on his sister. "I'm sorry."

"Wait..." She took a step back, and her forehead wrinkled. "Did you just apologize to me?"

"Yeah, I should've told you. Honestly, I was so focused on Mia and keeping her family updated that I didn't purposely mean to leave you out." He shrugged his shoulders. "It's just when you get upset, you kind of get loud."

"Yes, Liam, when I was ten, I'd get loud." Bree shook her head and pursed her lips. "But I'm twenty now and have grown up from there. You probably haven't realized it since you and Dad keep trying to treat me like a little girl who needs to be controlled."

Most likely this particular conversation had been coming for some time. My kidnapping had been the catalyst to finally bring it to the surface.

"You're right." Liam nodded. "I'll do better in the future."

A genuine smile spread across her face. "That sounds like a plan."

"Who were you talking to?" Whoever it was, they had been talking about me.

"Oh, Kai." She chewed on her bottom lip. "He's on his way over here. I hope that's okay."

"She's still hurting," Liam growled as he took my hand in his.

"I'm feeling better." I forced a smile. I wasn't lying, but it wasn't like I was feeling normal either. "I'm actually hungry."

"What do you want?" Liam pulled his phone out of his pocket. "I can order you something and pick it up."

"A pizza with all the meats sounds good." My stomach rumbled at the thought. Apparently, I hadn't eaten in four days except for toast and some saltine crackers a few hours ago.

"Okay." He stepped toward me and brushed his lips against mine. "I'm on it. Go sit down and rest." He headed toward the kitchen.

Bree watched him. "It's like he's a different person."

"What do you mean?" He wasn't as angry as he was when we first bonded. It was something I'd been noticing a lot more the last several hours.

"He apologized to me and was nice." Bree shook her head and then focused on my left shoulder. "Is that the one that's shot? It still smells like it's bleeding."

I was exhausted but wasn't ready to lie down again, especially if Kai was going to be here at any moment. "It is a little, but not like it was. It's starting to scab over, so that's a good thing." I should be back to normal in the next three to four days.

"We've all been worried." Bree gave me a small smile.

"I didn't mean to cause problems." I headed over to the recliner and sat in the seat. It still hurt to move; granted, it was a lot better than yesterday. I hadn't realized how often I used the muscles in my shoulders until now.

"It'll be ready in fifteen minutes." Liam breezed back into the room and stopped beside my recliner. "Do you need anything now?"

He'd been pushing me to down liquids all morning, so I wasn't thirsty. Just the thought of drinking more water right now made my stomach hurt. Honestly, I couldn't figure out how I was still hungry seeing as my stomach was filled with water. "No, I'm good. Thank you."

There was a brief knock on the door.

Liam stiffened ever so slightly as he took a deep breath. He hurried over to the door and opened it, revealing both Kai and Tripp standing there.

Tripp's eyes widened when he saw Liam. He lifted both hands in the air. "I never tried dating her."

"Really?" Kai rolled his eyes and took a deep breath. "You're going to throw me under the bus?"

"It's not like he doesn't already know." Tripp pointed to Liam. "You openly dated his mate right in front of him."

"You know, you two are making it hard for me to not want to hurt you right now," Liam growled deep.

"I didn't do anything. It was all him." Tripp pointed to Kai and raised both hands in the air as he slid past him and into the room.

"Wow, remind me never to tell Tripp something that could get me in trouble." Bree snorted and glanced at me. "He'll rat you out without any hesitation."

"Hey, he can kick my ass." Tripp pointed back at Liam. "I'm going to make it clear that my face doesn't need any rearrangements with his fist."

A laugh escaped me, and I cringed. It hurt so damn bad.

"Knock it off," Liam growled at him. "You made her hurt."

"It doesn't take much to get on his bad side." Bree winked at me. "Especially when it comes to Mia."

"How are you feeling?" Kai stepped to the side so he could see me, but he stayed in the entryway. "I've wanted to check on you but knew it probably wouldn't be good to come until you got back here."

"I'm okay." I tried to force a smile.

"She's lying. She's still hurting like hell." Liam shook his head and looked at me tenderly. "She doesn't want anyone to worry about her." He glanced at his phone and took a deep breath. "I'm going to go grab a pizza for her. Does anyone else want anything?"

Bree's eyebrows shot up, and Kai shuffled his feet.

Why is everyone looking at me all weird? Liam locked his eyes with mine. *I'm trying to be nice.*

A huge grin filled my face. *That's why.* "So, is that a no?"

"Oh, uh ... I wouldn't mind a pizza," Kai spoke his words carefully as if he was waiting for some type of punch line.

"I ordered five, so we should be good." He stepped out the door and waved Kai in. "I'll be back in a few minutes." His eyes focused back on me. "Let me know if you need anything. I won't be long."

I love you. I gave him a smile. He was trying for me and leaving Kai here without being an asshole. He was putting me before his own needs.

At this moment, I think it's pretty obvious how much I love you. He shut the door, and I could hear his footsteps down the hallway.

"What the hell just happened?" Tripp looked at me and then back at the door. "He just left you alone with us."

"He wasn't thrilled with it, but he did." Bree grinned at me. "I'll be honest. I had a gut feeling that you two were mates for a while, but I was happy when he left you alone. I was afraid he'd change you. Make you into one of those elitist bitches, but I can see now that isn't going to happen. You're bringing him back down to earth."

"I haven't asked him to change." Anything he was doing was all on him. I didn't deserve any of the credit.

"I hate to agree with Bree, but maybe fate did have it right after all." Kai sat on the recliner right across from me. "I can't believe you're up today. Hell, you were shot just a little over twenty-four hours ago."

"You do look like shit." Tripp frowned as he sat on the

other end of the couch. "You may be even paler than that huge heir that he hangs out with."

Bree leaned over and smacked Tripp on the arm. "That's not helping."

"No, it's fine." I didn't feel great, so I could only imagine what I looked like. I couldn't wait until my shoulder healed a little more so I could take a really good shower and maybe breathe without constant pain. "I don't feel the best though."

"How'd you get shot?" Tripp's eyes sparkled. "I've never known anyone who's gotten injured like that. I am officially a badass."

"How are you badass?" Kai scoffed and shook his head. "You're not the one who took the bullet."

"I'm a badass by association." Tripp patted himself on his chest as a proud grin spread across his face. "Everyone will fear me because they know I have an ace in my pocket."

"Oh, so we're friends again?" It sure seemed like he had been siding with Kai the last time we talked.

He grimaced. "Yeah, I'm sorry for being an ass."

I was thankful that we were fine now.

"If it wasn't for her, Micah wouldn't be alive right now." Kai gave me a sad smile.

"Wait. You saved one of those asshole heirs that beat your brother up?" Tripp's brows furrowed. "Why?"

"Because it was the right thing to do. And to be honest, everyone deserves a second chance." Maybe if he had killed my brother, I'd have felt differently ... but thankfully, I didn't have to worry about that. "And he was there to save me. He could've let the wolf he was attacking get me, but he didn't."

"Only because of Liam." Kai frowned.

"Yeah, but so what? He still didn't have to come." That also applied to Simon even though he had to be half crazy.

There was no telling what he had gone through while being raised by one of the council members. A while ago, I'd started to see that the heirs weren't raised by loving and caring fathers. Now that I thought about it, I'd never seen nor heard mention of their mothers. "This is kind of random, but why don't you guys ever mention your mom?"

"That, my friend, is a sad story." Bree sat back in her seat and frowned. "Mom isn't the most loving. She's either at home in her room away from us or out with her friends. The only time she comes around is for events where she is required to be present with Dad." Bree sighed. "She wasn't really around to raise us. Dad wanted the responsibility."

"Why does it have to be one or the other?" Tripp seemed to be hanging on her every word.

The heirs were viewed as strong and mysterious. We were getting a glimpse behind the veil.

"You have to understand the council members. All four of them," Bree said as she rubbed her hands together, "they refused their fated mates and forced a mate bond with women that they didn't care for. It was so the females didn't have any control over them. Most of the women, including my mother, weren't in it for raising a family. They were only in it for the benefits it gives them, and all they had to do was pop out an heir and a spare."

"I hadn't ever really thought about it that way, but you're right. It's almost like you're royalty." They'd need a spare in case something happened to the firstborn.

"Is your relationship with your mom that way?" Tripp focused on Kai.

"No, my mom is just as involved in my life as my dad." Kai shrugged his shoulders. "Even though they aren't fated, they still love each other. But I'm not an heir like those four are."

In times like these, it was crazy to think I was an heir to the council as well. I grew up so removed from this world, but I was learning more and more that was a good thing.

The front door opened, and Liam walked in, carrying the pizza with Evan right behind him.

As Liam headed to the kitchen to put the pizzas on the table, Evan closed the door and came straight to me.

"Let me take a look." His hands went to my shoulder and gently moved my shirt to the side. He looked at the bandage and frowned. "We need to change it out." Evan pulled out a bandage from his pocket and surgical tape.

Bree's mouth dropped open.

Liam walked back into the room with two plates of food and two bottles of water. He placed the drinks and plates on the table as Evan began carefully removing the tape.

"So we can touch her now?" Kai's eyes widened in surprise.

"He is helping her. However, you still have feelings for her." Liam's voice was raspy. "I really appreciated all of your help finding her, and that's why you're here. If it weren't for you, things could have turned out much differently. But let's not push anymore right now. I can only take so much."

"That's fair." Kai sucked in a deep breath.

My heart melted at Liam's words.

Soon, Evan removed all of the dressing and looked at my wound. "It's finally stopped bleeding."

"Shouldn't she be healing faster than that?" Bree leaned over so she could see my injury.

"Yeah, but it's in the same place that Simon hurt her. Plus, we had to dig the bullet out, so it's a pretty extensive injury to a previously injured area." He gently put another large bandage over it and began taping it up.

Even though he was being careful, it still hurt as he messed with it.

"How do you know all this?" Tripp pursed his lips as he watched.

"I'm majoring in pre-med." Evan put my shirt back in place and picked up the dirty bandage and tape from the chair. "So, I at least know the basics." He headed into the kitchen without another word. Turning the water on, he washed his hands.

You need to eat. Liam picked up both plates from the table and handed me one as he sat on the floor next to my recliner. *Do you need anything else?*

No, thank you. I used my right hand to eat so I didn't move the left one quite as much.

Evan entered the room again a few seconds later with his own plate and a bottle of medicine. "Here, it's time for your medicine too. Try to eat a little bit before taking it though. Your stomach could get upset."

A grin spread across Bree's face as she sat back and watched.

I took the pill and frowned. It was both a blessing and a curse. The last time I had to drink so much coffee to stay awake. "I don't want to get sleepy again. I feel like all I've done is sleep for the last few days."

"You need your rest." Evan sat in front of the table and pointed at me. "You'll heal faster that way."

"Fine." The pain was coming back with a vengeance, so it didn't take too much coaxing on his part. I popped the pill in my mouth and took a sip of water.

There was silence until Bree stood up and waved to the guys. "I'm starving. Let's grab some food too."

I enjoyed the quiet of the moment as the six of us settled in for a quick meal.

It wasn't long before my eyes grew heavy and I laid my head back on the headrest.

We need to get you to bed. Liam placed his plate back on the coffee table and stood up at the same time as Kai and Tripp.

"Thanks for dinner, but I think we'd better leave." Kai smiled at me. "You look like you might pass out any moment just sitting there."

Between the food and the medicine, I was barely able to keep my eyes open. "Thanks for coming to visit."

"Let's get you to bed." Liam glanced over at Evan. "I'll be staying here tonight."

"Figured you would." Evan reached for the plates when Bree got up and smacked his hands. "Go on. I've got this."

As I stood, I winced in pain.

Dammit, I feel helpless. There is no way I can help you. I'm worried that I'd only make you hurt worse. He took my hand, and we headed toward the hallway.

"Thanks for coming, guys. I'll see you soon." I tried smiling, but it fell short.

Moments later, we were walking into my bedroom, and I immediately laid down on the bed. Liam shut the door and crawled up next to me.

We lay there in silence as he brushed his fingertips along my arm, relaxing me. Moments like these were rare and too fleeting.

All of a sudden, there was a pounding on the front door.

Bree opened the door, and Micah's familiar voice filled the room. "Where is Liam?"

"Where the hell do you think he is?" Bree's voice was

short and sounded annoyed. "You can't just go into her room."

"It's not like they'll be doing anything." Micah banged on our door. "She's too hurt for anything like that."

"I wasn't talking about sex, idiot." Bree's voice was low and growly. "I was talking about rest."

Liam's body tensed. "Come in, but it better be good."

The door opened, and Micah entered. When his golden eyes landed on me, he paused. "I'm so sorry you're hurt." He cleared his throat and took another hesitant step into the room. "I didn't get the chance to say thank you, so... uh... thank you."

I couldn't stop the smile from spreading across my face. "You're welcome, but let's try not to let this happen again. Okay?"

Micah chuckled. "Deal."

"This is why you came in here?" Liam scowled at Micah. "You could've waited till tomorrow."

"No, I found out who helped get Mia kidnapped." Micah took a deep breath and stared Liam in the eyes. "It was Amber."

My heart dropped, but the words made sense now that he said them. She had purposely gotten me to follow her. If that bitch thought she had gotten the upper hand, she was about to learn how far she could fall.

CHAPTER NINE

The alarm sounded, and my eyes flew open. Instantly, the pain hit again. The only reason I slept any last night was due to the painkillers Evan gave me.

"I'll go meet the guys. You get some rest." Liam was spooning me, and he lifted himself over my shoulder to kiss my cheek.

"No, I want to go too." I turned on to my back, and tears threatened my eyes as the pain sliced through my shoulder.

"Are you okay?" The concern was clear in his voice.

"Yeah, I'm not hurting near as bad." I yanked the covers off me and sat up slowly. Yes, it hurt, but not the mind-numbing pain it had been. "I want to go too. I need to be there. I can't look weak."

"You took a fucking bullet." He shook his head and sat next to me. "You don't look weak at all."

"Maybe, but I'm not hurting like I was, so I'm coming. I'll take some Advil instead of the strong painkillers that make me want to sleep all day." Now that I could somewhat move, I needed to get back to class.

I got up and went into my closet, selecting a silver Wolf

Moon Academy polo shirt and a blood-red academy skirt. It was getting colder now that it was October, so I grabbed a pair of silver leggings to wear underneath.

Liam was already dressed in his blood-red shirt and khakis. "At least, let me help you get dressed." When he turned and saw what I chose, he shook his head. "You're planning on going to class, aren't you?"

"Well, yeah." The longer I stayed out, the more I was getting behind. Also, I felt a little trapped and needed to get some fresh air and do something different. "I need to go."

He blew out a breath and shook his head. "Fine, but I'm carrying your stuff to each one. There's no way you can wear a backpack, and it's only fair since I think it's still too early."

"That's fair." The fact that he listened meant the world to me. He was afraid for me to be away from him, so this was taking a lot for him. However, we needed the practice since he'd be gone all of fall break.

"Here, let me help you." He walked over and took hold of the edges of my shirt, helping me slowly take it off. I still wasn't able to raise my arm, so he helped pull my arm out before pulling the shirt completely off. It took a minute, but soon I had the polo shirt on. He also helped change me into my leggings and skirt. "I never thought I'd see the day where I was helping you dress. I figured I would always be undressing you." Even though he was attempting a joke, the anxiety coming through our bond made it clear he was struggling with me being hurt like this.

"Give me a day or two and I'll be ready to make up for lost time." I stood on my tiptoes and pressed my lips to his.

"I'll be counting down the minutes." He kissed me back and pinched my ass.

"Hey." I laughed, and for once, it didn't feel like I got

stabbed in the shoulder. "Do you mind brushing my hair?" Even though my right shoulder was fine, any movement like that also pulled the muscles in my injured shoulder. I wasn't ready to be that tough yet.

"Of course." He grabbed the brush and ran it through my hair.

After rushing into the bathroom, I brushed my teeth, put a little bit of makeup on to give my cheeks some color, and used the bathroom before I was ready to start the day. I headed back into my room to find Liam texting on his phone.

He glanced up and met my eyes. "Are you ready? The guys are at my dorm, waiting on us."

"Yeah." I hadn't meant to make him late, but I couldn't leave looking like I'd just rolled out of bed.

His face spread into a grin. "You do look like you're feeling better."

"I am, but the makeup also helps hide some of the pain." I pointed to my backpack against the wall. "Do you mind carrying it?"

"If you remember, I told you that was a requirement." He winked at me and grabbed the bag. He opened the door and waved me through. "Evan's cooking French toast."

"Wait. Really?" That was my favorite breakfast meal, and the restaurant didn't have it on the menu. Apparently, I'd talked in my sleep while recovering in their dorm room. Both Evan and Liam had fun listening.

"I don't know if I should be ecstatic that Evan likes you or jealous." He shook his head. "He's never gotten up to make me breakfast before."

"Stop. He knows we're fated mates." I walked down the hallway to the front door. "You've got nothing to be concerned with. Hell, he was the one who told me to leave with you the night of the party."

"That's his only saving grace. Well, that, and he knew how to get the bullet out and take care of you." He arched an eyebrow as he opened the door.

Soon, we were outside the building and walking into his dorm next door. By the time we entered their room, Evan was laying a plate on their kitchen table with the pill bottle next to it. Micah and Simon were giving him strange looks as they sat on the couch.

That piece of furniture was the one slight change from their dorm and mine and Bree's. They had a more open floor plan where the kitchen table was open to the den.

"What's she doing here?" Simon's amber eyes scanned me over as he scowled in my direction. His skin wasn't as dark as Micah's but a slightly darker olive tone than mine and Liam's; his ash-blond hair made him appear darker. His body tensed as he wrinkled his nose.

"Who'd you think I made French toast for?" Evan rolled his eyes.

"Wait. You did that for her? I thought it was for you." Simon looked at each one of the heirs, stopping on Micah. "Tell them this is ridiculous."

"She saved my life, man." Micah lifted both hands in the air. "So..."

"Are you fucking serious?" Simon took a step back and shook his head. "You've all lost your damn minds." He pointed at me. "Her dad's not even a city alpha. What the hell are you three thinking?"

"We aren't here to debate this." Liam placed my bag on the floor and went over to the table, pulling the seat out for me. "Eat and take the meds. You need to stay on top of the pain."

He didn't have to tell me twice. I dug my fork into the French toast and took a bite. "Ooh, it's delicious." I turned to Evan. "Tastes just like my mom's."

"That's because we got her recipe." Liam chuckled as he watched me.

"You need the medicine." Evan pointed at the bottle.

"I just want Advil today. I want to go to class." I took another bite of the food and enjoyed the taste.

Evan eyed Liam as if he was asking permission.

"Oh, no." I pointed at Evan and lifted my head. I didn't care if I had a mouthful of food, they didn't get to make my decisions for me. "This isn't something the two of you decide for me. I refuse to take this damn pill, so give me the stuff I'm asking for."

"Just do it." Liam nodded his head, and Evan headed back into the kitchen, opened a cabinet, and pulled out the medicine. He brought me four pills. "Here."

"Thank you." I glanced around the room. "Is anyone else going to eat?" It felt strange that all four of them were watching me stuff my face.

"Yeah, I made enough for all of us." Evan went back to the kitchen and piled his plate full while Liam and Micah followed his lead.

When Simon stood from the couch, he just stared at the four of us sitting at the table. He shook his head. "So, we're just a happy fucking family now. We all come together to eat breakfast and talk about our day?"

"Shut the hell up, Simon." Liam turned his chair so Simon wasn't to his back. "You know why we're all here, so get on with the story."

"With her here?" Simon blinked, and his mouth dropped open.

It appeared that we were going to have this same

conversation with him over and over again. "You might as well get used to my presence. If being kidnapped and shot didn't run me off, then it finally should sink in that I'm not going anywhere."

"She's right." Liam took a bite of his food as if he didn't have a care in the world, but our bond told a different story. He was pissed. "And if you try forcing our hand, then you'll be down an heir."

"Fine. Amber and I have been having a casual thing." Simon's eyes filled with laughter, and he smirked as he caught my eye. "You know, kinky sex. She still yells Liam's name sometimes, but I don't give a fuck."

Liam jumped out of his chair and grabbed Simon by the throat, holding him in the air just where his feet couldn't touch the ground. "I'm about to lose my shit. When Micah told us Amber helped in getting Mia kidnapped, all I wanted to do was go to her room and make her hurt like she'd done Mia. The only reason I didn't was because Mia needed rest, but today is a new day. And from here on out, if anyone tries to hurt her, they better be ready to feel my wrath. Do you understand?"

He nodded his head, and Liam placed his feet back on the ground.

"Got it." He rubbed his neck where Liam's handprint marked his flesh red. He cleared his throat as he took in a deep breath.

Liam walked back to his seat and popped another piece of food into his mouth as if what he'd just done was nothing. However, he was still livid. It had taken every bit of his control to put Simon down. Our bond didn't allow there to be any secrets between us.

It was crazy how I'd already forgotten how he could be. Granted, he never hurt me physically, but he had left some emotional scars before we finally worked things out between us.

"Now, please continue." Liam arched his eyebrow as if he was almost daring him.

"Like I was saying. Amber and I had been spending some time together. Yesterday, she asked where you've been. That she'd expected to see you by now." Simon sat on the couch and rubbed at his neck again. "I asked her what she meant. The bitch actually thought I was jealous." He chuckled.

Evan kept staring at me, so I finally gave in and took the four pills. He nodded and placed his focus on Simon as soon as I'd finished swallowing. At this point, I wasn't sure if he or Liam was worse.

"When I mentioned that you," Simon said as he pointed at Liam, "were taking care of Mia, that she'd gotten kidnapped and then hurt, Amber started freaking out."

"What do you mean, freaking out?" Evan's voice was his usual low rasp.

"She jumped up, got dressed, and started pacing, asking questions like 'did we know who took her'." Simon rolled his eyes. "She was upset, and I knew better than to believe she actually cared about someone so use..." He paused and winced. "So important to Liam."

"Did she come right out and say it?" Liam arched an eyebrow. "Or did you just assume it?"

"Well, she asked if we figured out who took her, and I said yes. That's when she broke down and told me that she was the one who had lured Mia into the trap. She kept going too, telling me that she and I needed to work together to get rid of her for good."

Wait. He does want to get rid of me for good, so why is he telling us this? It made no sense to me whatsoever.

It's because he's trying to use this as leverage over us.
Liam took a drink of his water, acting as if he didn't have a
care in the world. *He's using this information to make up for
hurting your brother. Evan and I haven't been talking to him,
and because of that, his father has been throwing a fit at the
council's meetings over it. He's trying to bridge the gap he
created between us. Especially now that Micah has crossed
over to our side.*

How can you all live like this? It still blew my mind.
They were heirs and vital to the shifter world. Yet, instead
of working together for the betterment of the packs, they
were scheming, trying to be the one with the most control
and power.

Honestly, I never questioned it before you. Through our
bond, I could feel his love and adoration. *It's always been
like this, how we were raised.* "So how did you respond?"

"I told her definitely. That the bitch needed to go."

Liam stood from his seat, ready to inflict pain once
more.

"Whoa!" Simon raised both hands in the air. "Obviously,
it's not going to happen even if I think it should, so I figured
I could lead Amber into some sort of trap."

"Did she say whether the council was involved?" Micah
took the last bite of his food. "Those three guys swore it was
them."

"No, and if our dads said they didn't do it, then we know
they didn't." Simon shrugged. "But if I play this right, then
maybe we can find out who really did order it."

Is he really that stupid? Who else would it have been? I
didn't see how Simon could believe them without any
hesitation.

*We were raised not to question them, and honestly, I
didn't have a reason to do so ... until you.* Liam nodded his

head. "Then, we use it. We can't do too much too soon, or she'll be suspicious. I want her ass in jail, so we need to get proof and show our dads. Then, we can get justice."

"That's cold." Simon grinned, and despite his words, humor filled his eyes. "She'll go down, taking her family with her. I fucking love it."

He scares the shit out of me. I'd always thought the other three were the scariest, but now I realized it was Simon. He was unhinged and enjoyed inflicting pain on others. Someone like him should never be allowed on the council.

There's nothing to be afraid of. Liam reached over and took my hand. *He's crazy but totally predictable.*

"That just proves I need to go back to class." I took the last bite of my food and stood. "If I go back and act normal, that will drive her even more crazy."

"I hate to admit it, but she has a point." Liam picked up my plate along with his and took them into the kitchen. "The quicker we go back to acting normal, the more irrational she'll get."

"Thank you for breakfast." I smiled at Evan, touched that he would do something like that for me.

"You're welcome." He stood and arched an eyebrow. "Be careful. Otherwise, you're going to be in a lot of pain tonight."

"Got it." I took a deep breath as Liam grabbed my bag and opened the door for me.

Here it was. I was returning to reality. I'd thought I was ready for it. However, after hearing how desperate Amber was to get rid of me, it made me hesitate. Except, I couldn't let fear dictate my life. Instead, I took a deep breath and exited the dorm to face my enemies head-on.

CHAPTER TEN

W hen we walked into the building that housed my Composition, Precalculus, and Shifter History classes, Liam sped up as we breezed through the main entrance between the stairwells. As we entered the hallway, he stepped slightly in front of me.

Before I could ask what he was doing, I heard *her* voice. "Liam, I've been worried about you. You missed the football game and haven't been around lately."

You missed your football game? That hadn't even crossed my mind. I had gone missing on a Thursday and they found me Saturday. They had a game against another smaller shifter school last weekend, and it was a huge deal.

Of course, I did. Evan did too. Do you really think I'd choose football over finding you? Liam stiffened and turned to face the bitch head-on. "Had more important plans last weekend." His feeling of hatred toward her filled our bond. He was so close to coming unglued.

"More important than a football game where packs came to see the heirs in action? Your dad was beside himself." A smile began to spread across her face until I stepped into her view.

I wasn't going to hide behind Liam. He wanted to protect me, but that was only going to make things worse. My wolf was as strong as his was, and we had to fight our battles together.

"As newly fated mates, I had more important things to do like spend time with Mia." His eyes were so dark that the navy blue could have easily been black. He looked at me and winked.

"Oh, well ..." She frowned, and her nose wrinkled in disgust. "I told you she's not good enough for you. Now she's got you missing important games."

"Football isn't what I'm concerned with." He gently wrapped his arm around my waist, careful not to jar my shoulder. "I've learned that there is more to life than being the quarterback." A tender smile crossed his face.

"It's more than a game, and you know it." She sneered as her gaze landed on me. "This is about all the packs seeing how strong and determined the heirs are. That's why you need someone like me by your side, who understands these things ... not her."

"Well, I'm not interested in having you." Liam narrowed his eyes and smirked. "But congratulations on snagging Simon. You two are perfect for each other."

"If that's what's holding you back, I can dump him in a heartbeat." She wet her bottom lip and scanned him from top to bottom like a piece of meat.

"It's cute that you think he'd want you." I'd never felt such hatred for someone before, and to be honest, I didn't like it at all.

"I wasn't talking to you." Her voice was a hiss as she spoke low.

"You need to get it into that dense head of yours." He dropped his hand from my waist and took a menacing step toward her while looking down his nose. "I was never yours, to begin with. Now, leave me alone. I won't be so kind if you try this shit one more time with either her or me." He turned his back on her and took my hand, pulling me toward the elevator.

Once we got in, he blew out a breath. *Damn! I'm so sorry.*

For what? He'd done absolutely nothing to apologize for.

Bringing you into this world. He stepped into me and brushed his fingers along my cheek. *It's like around every corner, someone is there who wants to hurt us.*

You didn't bring me into this world. I'd be here regardless. He needed to remember that I was an heir too. *You do realize I'll be taking back what is mine?*

A huge smile spread across his face. *Damn straight, you will. There's no one I'd rather work next to, and we'll make sure you assume your rightful place on the council. We just have to be careful and take our time.*

That, I could do. Even though it was something I wanted so very badly, it could wait. At the moment, there was too much going on, and we needed to make sure my secret was revealed at the proper time. Whenever that may be.

He took my hand as the elevator doors opened, and he pulled me toward my classroom. As soon as we walked through the door, Tripp, Robyn, and her two followers, along with another guy glanced at us. Robyn's eyes narrowed on Liam and my joined hands.

"Ugh ... I had hoped you'd come to your senses by now." Robyn shook her head as her nose wrinkled in disgust. "Or is it just that you want to fuck the nobodies before settling down with a real woman?"

"Do you mean a real woman or a brown-noser who's had their head so far up someone's ass that she can't smell anything other than shit?" I batted my eyelashes and grinned.

"You better watch it." Robyn stood from her desk in the middle of the front row. "Do you have any idea who my father is?"

"No, you better watch it," Liam growled, his eyes glowing with his wolf coming forward. "I could take your father down so fast it's not funny. One more word, and it'll happen."

Robyn frowned but didn't sit down.

"You'd better sit down." Her friend, Olivia, said as her pale green eyes widened. "He's not kidding around."

"Fine." Robyn huffed and reluctantly sat in her seat. Her body was tight with anger.

I brushed past her and sat at my desk right behind her and next to Tripp.

"Hey, man." Tripp smiled at Liam. "How's our badass doing?" His eyes landed on me and winked. "How am I not surprised she's here today?"

"Because she's strong." Liam bent down and kissed my cheek as he placed my backpack at my feet.

"And stubborn." Tripp pointed at me like his fingers were guns. "I bet you didn't have any say to her being here."

"Damn right about that." Liam chuckled.

"You two realize I'm sitting right here." They were both picking at me, but I hated to be talked about as if I wasn't there.

"Hey, we're just kidding." Liam squeezed my hand

gently. *I'm really trying to get along with your friends. That's all. I know they're important to you.*

Still not happy about getting picked on. I arched an eyebrow at him.

He chuckled and glanced back at Tripp. "Make sure she stays here after class until I can get back down here."

"Will do." Tripp saluted him.

I love you. He kissed the top of my head and turned, heading out of the classroom.

"He's like a different person now." Tripp shook his head as he watched Liam disappear into the mass of people.

"No, that's always been him." He was an amazing person, and now people were finally seeing it. "He just got lost along the way for a little while."

I LEANED BACK in the passenger seat of Liam's car and closed my eyes as we headed toward my parents' house. We'd woken up early to visit them since Liam needed to get back at a decent hour to pack for his week tour of some of the large cities with the other heirs.

We'd hoped to go Saturday, but he had a late football game that he didn't need to miss, especially since he had skipped the one last week. For once, I enjoyed the game and got to hang out with Bree, Tripp, and Kai without any drama. After the game, Liam and Evan joined us back at my dorm to watch some movies and celebrate their win.

"It's nice seeing you relax and not wincing in pain every few seconds." Liam reached over and took my hand in his. "I was so damn scared you weren't going to make it."

In all reality, it took longer than I'd expected to heal. I had been more injured than we initially thought, and Evan said I was damn lucky I survived. Honestly, I'd almost succumbed to the darkness, and it was only because of Liam that I didn't. He had saved me. "Well, it didn't happen, and we're together. That's all that matters." Today was the first day that I didn't have much pain. The shoulder still bothered me if I moved suddenly, but not anything compared to how I was that first night in Evan and Liam's dorm room. It had hurt just to breathe.

The rest of the ride was spent in companionable silence, and soon Liam was pulling up to my parents' house.

The front door opened with both Mom and Dad rushing out the door and heading over to me.

Dad opened my door, causing his blue shirt to bunch on his shoulders, and then held his hand out. "Here, let me help you."

The concern and love on their faces warmed my heart. "I'm better now. You don't have to help me."

"Let your father help you." Mom narrowed her caramel eyes at me and crossed her arms. "We've been beside ourselves this past week. The only saving grace for me and your dad not showing up on campus and throwing a fit is because of your mate. So if your dad wants to help you get out of the damn car, you can let him."

Damn, now I see where you get your strength. Liam chuckled as he climbed out of the car and shut his door.

Dad took my arm and helped me get out of the car. He actually made my shoulder twinge in pain by assisting me, but I wasn't going to let him know. "Thank you."

"It's nice to see you again, Mr. And Mrs. Davis." Liam nodded his head at them and smiled.

He was a completely different person than the last time he came here. Granted, we had been here on a learning expedition and had only just completed our mate bond.

"Oh, after everything you've done, you're getting a hug."
Mom hurried over to him and wrapped her arms around
him. "I don't know what would've happened if it weren't for
you."

Liam hugged her back, and his cheeks turned a slight
pink. "I didn't do anything."

"You took care of our daughter when we couldn't." Dad
walked over and shook Liam's hand. "Last time we met you,
it wasn't under the best of circumstances. But this time, I'd
like to say welcome to the family."

"Thank you." Liam scratched the back of his neck as he
glanced in my direction. Through our bond, I could tell he
was happy but uncomfortable. He wasn't used to being
treated this way.

The front door opened again, and Max stuck his head
out. "You better get your ass in here before I eat all the
cinnamon rolls." He held one up so I could see and took a
huge bite out of it.

"You better not." I hadn't had Mom's cooking in so long,
and those baked treats were one of my favorites. I hurried
inside and ran to the left, down the narrow hallway,
following the decadent cinnamon smell of home. When I
saw the hot pan of ten cinnamon rolls, I picked up two and
took a large bite. The taste was heavenly, and I hated to
admit it, but I moaned.

I'm not sure if I should be jealous or not. Liam entered
the room behind my parents and smiled when he saw me.
He reached for one of the treats in my hand, and I jerked
my hand out of his reach.

"Uh-uh; Get your own," I growled through a mouthful
of vanilla frosting and cinnamon.

"Why are you encouraging him to eat any?" Max

frowned as he popped the last bite of the one he had been eating and went for another.

"You two, stop it." Mom giggled even though she tried to school her face into an indifferent expression. "He can have some too."

"I'm not sure that I can." Liam laughed. "I might get bitten."

"Looks like Mia has already done that to you." Max pointed to the faint scar of teeth marks on his neck.

"Maximum Davis." Mom pointed at him and frowned. "Please don't ever point that out to me again."

"What? You know they're mates." Max whined as he grabbed two more cinnamon rolls before walking away with his head hung in shame.

"You'd better get some before they're gone." Dad made his way to the pan and grabbed one for himself. "Those two are vicious and will eat them all if given the chance."

"Well, if they're as good as they're making them out to be, I just might need to take two." Liam winked at me and grabbed two.

"This is all on you." Max pointed at me. "You had to go get mated, so now we have to share our food."

Mom watched the whole interaction with the biggest smile on her face.

"So, Max and I are going to watch some football in the living room." Dad glanced at Liam. "Do you want to join us?"

Liam walked over next to me so our arms were touching. *Mind if I go in there so you and your mom can have some alone time? I'm assuming that's what your dad is getting at.*

Go if you want to. I'd never thought my parents would be so welcoming to him. After the way Mom had reacted when I told her about who my mate was, and considering how everything went down the last time I was here, I kind of gave up on my family being okay with our bond. *I'll be fine. She is my mother after all.*

"Sure, let's go see who is playing." Liam's eyes were light blue, which was rare for me to see. He crammed a cinnamon roll in his mouth and grabbed another one while talking with his mouth full. "But let me grab another one of these before we leave the kitchen."

Max growled and scowled at me. "This is on you."

Dad laughed. "Well, all right then." Dad finished his food, waving Liam and Max toward the living room. "Let's go and give these two some alone time. Come join us when you ladies are done."

The three of them rushed out of the kitchen, leaving Mom and me behind.

"Really, I'm the winner here. I have direct access to the rest." I grabbed the last cinnamon roll and made my way to the rectangular table that was in the corner of the kitchen. I sat in one of the seats and got comfortable.

"One second. I'll be right back." Mom disappeared into the living room.

I got up and opened the stainless steel refrigerator and pulled out a bottle of water. As I settled back into my spot at the table, Mom came back in with a picture album.

As she took the seat next to me, she gave me a grin. "I was wrong about him."

"Liam?" I didn't want to say too much and ruin whatever she wanted to tell me.

"Yes. I'll be honest; I'm not thrilled that you're at that school. When you told me that he was your fated mate, it petrified me. The night you came here and he was so guarded and angry, I thought it proved my point even more.

But he was so good to call us and let us know everything. The pain in his voice — that was when I realized he really does love you. And seeing him here, I'm glad fate chose him."

"Even though he's an heir to the council?" The last few times I'd talked to Mom, she was acting normal. I'd hoped it hadn't been a fluke, and her words eased some of my worry.

"Honey, I've come to realize it doesn't matter. At the end of the day, you're an heir just as much as he is, and fate has a way of unveiling hidden truths." She opened up the picture album and caressed one of the photos. "You were meant for great things just like your father was." She turned the photo album toward me.

My breath caught in my throat as I stared at a man who was a complete stranger but also seemed familiar. His emerald eyes that matched my own stared back at me, and like me, his hair was as black as the night. "Is that him?"

"Yes, that's your biological father, Brent Forrest." Her eyes filled with tears as she stared at him. "The love of my life who was stolen way too soon."

"Why are you showing me this?" I didn't know how, but this made everything seem so much more real. He now had a face and one that I would see every time I looked in the mirror. I wasn't sure if I was happy to be able to picture him or if it somehow made the whole thing worse.

"Because you need to know your heritage. I know I tried keeping it from you, but it took seeing Liam treating you like a mate and you getting hurt to make me realize I'm not in control. That, in fact, I was actually hurting you. By not sharing him with you, I didn't let you in on something that you have every right to know about." She flipped the page again. "Unfortunately, Brent's parents died shortly after he took over the seat of the council. That's when the other council members became more to him. They were his second family until he met me. The five heirs were inseparable growing up."

I glanced at the page and found five faces smiling at us. It was easy to pick out who was who. Simon's dad had that California glow like his son did. Micah's skin was just as dark as his father's, and both Mr. Rafferty and Mr. Hale looked nearly the same as they did now. It was almost as if they hadn't aged.

When she turned the page again, her eyes clouded with tears. "This was right after our claiming ceremony." The picture was a younger version of her with him on a beach. He had her scooped up in his arms, and they were looking at each other with love written across their faces. She wore a simple white dress, and he was in a black suit. The waves crashed behind them as though the ocean was applauding their love.

"You two were so happy." If I had any doubts that she loved him, they were gone now.

"That's how you and Liam look at each other." She wiped a tear from under her eye and gave me a sad smile. "I still dream about this day. Sometimes, I wake up smelling the salt in the air as if I were still there."

"I'm sorry." I didn't know what else to say. I couldn't imagine not having Liam in my life. If he were to die, I didn't know if I could be strong enough to move on like she'd done.

"I won't lie. I miss him just as much as the day I realized he wasn't coming home." Her shoulders shook. "But know that with Ethan, Max, and you, I was able to find a sense of happiness, despite it all. What I'm trying to say is to cherish Liam. I was wrong for telling you to reject him. Cherish him and love him with all your heart. One day, he might not be there, and I don't want you to have any regrets like I do." She sniffed and turned the page again.

It was her in a room that had Wolf Moon Academy's school colors with my dad bent down with his head on her belly. "That was when we knew we were having you. He set up a camera to capture the moment together." She smashed her lips together as tears poured down her cheeks. "He was so excited. Your heartbeat was on the higher end, so we knew you were a girl. I was afraid he'd be upset when we realized you were a girl and not a boy. He shook his head no without hesitation on his face. He said it was fitting since the original Overseer had been a woman, and he hoped you looked just like me." Her laugh was between a strangle and a cry. "And here you are, the spitting image of him."

"Mom, we don't have to do this." My heart was aching, not only over the man I never got to know but because my mother was breaking down in front of me. She had never done that before.

What's wrong? Liam's concerned voice linked in my mind. *Do you need me?*

No, I'm okay. Mom is showing me pictures of my father. It wasn't fair that dad had been taken from us. He didn't get to live near long enough. *I've never seen him before.*

"Here is one last picture that I have." She flipped to another page, and I blinked several times. There, beside my father, stood a man who appeared to be several years older than him. He looked like my professor for Shifter History 101. "Who is that?" *Liam, you need to come in here.* I opened the bond so he could hear what my mother was saying.

"Ah, that's your grandmother's brother. I'd heard he was the last living relative of your father." She gave me a sad smile. "He was never in line for the council seat because it was from Brent's mother's side. The lineage came down from your grandfather's family tree."

Liam walked into the kitchen and to my side. "What's wrong?"

I pointed at the picture. "He's my history professor." It had to be him. The man looked just like him. "Professor Johnson."

"I'm not sure. I never got to meet him, but your father said he hated the council and everything it stood for. It was a point of contention between your grandparents." Mom's face filled with pain. "And honestly, your father and I had only a month together. Most of it was spent with the two of us caught up in each other."

"So that's why they are keeping him as faculty." Liam laughed, but it was without humor. "I always wondered why they kept him on when Dad and the others hated him so much."

"What do you mean?" I wasn't following his logic.

"Sometimes it's best to keep your enemies close." Liam's eyes darkened like they did with anything that dealt with his father or the council. "That's one reason why we heirs would always hang out together. Stay close so you can monitor and threaten if needed."

"So, they are keeping him close so he can't speak horribly of the council." Mom shook her head and took in a deep breath. "Trying to control what message he spreads into the world."

"If you think that's bad, you don't want to know everything." Liam met my eyes. *Something isn't right, and we need to get to the bottom of it.*

His words scared me. They weren't anything I hadn't thought of myself, but this was the first time he'd said the words and meant them with every fiber of his being.

CHAPTER ELEVEN

S oon after we finished dinner with the family, we were back in Liam's car, returning to Wolf Moon Academy.

"I'm a little surprised, but I had a great time." Liam reached over and took my hand in his. "Your family is so supportive and loving."

"And they love you too." Going back there today had been better than I could ever have expected. At dinner, my parents told embarrassing stories about me and what Liam had gotten himself into. We had laughed so much that my sides had started hurting.

"I'm damn lucky to have found you. I never had that growing up." He gave me a sad smile. "We would eat dinner together at night. But it mostly consisted of what Bree or I needed to do better and to learn etiquette. If we did have a general conversation, it was around council business and how the packs needed to stop complaining so much. They had it so much better than years past."

"I'm sure you and Bree had fun together." Bree had a great sense of humor and was as loyal as they came.

"She's always been a pleaser though." Liam squeezed my

hand. "Dad was always focused on me and who I had to become. Bree tried to do anything to get his attention. She went out of her way to get great grades and be the daughter she thought he wanted. That's one reason why she fights her bond with Nate."

"Like someone else I know." I arched an eyebrow. He'd fought our bond for almost two months. "And why am I not surprised you figured out they were mates?"

"Because, I pick up on things. And you and me, well that was different." He narrowed his eyes at me. "And you know it. I thought I was putting you in danger." He paused and held up a finger on his left hand, which was on the steering wheel. "Correction, I've put you in danger."

"Not any more than I'll be when the truth comes out, and besides, you're worth it." I leaned back in my seat and closed my eyes. Even though I was better, I still got tired easily.

"Take a nap. I'll wake you up when we get home." Liam's voice was deep and comforting.

For once, I didn't mind listening to him, and I faded into sleep.

As WE CLIMBED out of Liam's car, he stepped around to my side and took my hand. "Come on, let's get you packed before we head over to my dorm. We need to sleep there tonight so we don't wake Bree up in the morning. You know how she is."

"Wait. Why am I getting packed?" I'd been avoiding thinking about him leaving me for a week and purposely had steered clear of that conversation with him. I was afraid

I'd guilt him into staying, and that was the last thing I wanted to do.

"Because we travel in the morning." He arched an eyebrow at me, and then he nodded his head as if realization had sunk in. "Did you really think I would leave you behind unprotected?"

"No ... I mean I was going to stay on campus and not follow anyone, especially Amber, anywhere." The thought of going with him excited me, but I didn't want him to feel obligated to take me.

"I'm not going without you." He stopped and turned my body to face him. "So if you don't want to go, say the word."

"I don't want to cause more problems between you and your father." At the end of the day, Mr. Hale was still his dad.

"Do you really think there could be anything else that got in between us?" Liam raised an eyebrow. *He tries to control me. He tried to keep me from mating with you, and he hired mercenaries to kidnap you. Hell, I have no clue what their plans at the end of that fiasco were for you. He doesn't have my best interests at heart, and I'm starting to have my doubts about whether he should actually be in power. I don't trust him with you, and honestly, I don't want to go anywhere without you by my side. So are we going, or are we staying home for the week?*

He won't let me on the plane. I could only imagine his reaction when I showed up.

He won't be there. That's one reason why we're going so early. Evan scheduled it with the sole purpose of you going with us. After all, we are really just following his directions. All the heirs are to go on this trip, and you are, in fact, an heir too. You need to see all this just as much as the four of us.

It would be helpful for me later, especially since I

would wind up being a council member. *Okay, let's go.* I hadn't ever gotten to travel before, so this was exciting. Not only that, but we'd get to meet other wolves and see what kind of problems their packs had.

Good, now let's go get your stuff. He took my hand and led me inside the dorm. When we entered the room, Bree was pulling two large suitcases behind her.

"Where are you going?" Liam's forehead wrinkled as his eyes landed on the suitcases.

"I'm... uh..." Bree looked at me and cringed.

"She's going home with Nate to meet his family." He had to get over not wanting them to be together.

"Like hell she is..." He growled.

"Oh, shut it." I rolled my eyes and stepped in front of him. "He's her fated, and she has just as much right to be with him as you do with me. So stop acting like your father."

It was like he deflated right before my eyes. His shoulders sagged, and he stared at the ground. "I am, aren't I?"

"Don't you want her to be happy?" I walked over to Bree and wrapped my arm around her shoulders. "She deserves to have what we have. Do you want to keep pushing her, making her feel like you did when you were trying to reject me?"

Bree let go of one of her bags, which had been rolling behind her, and wrapped her free arm around me as well.

"God, no." He ran a hand through his short, dark hair. "Fine, go. But don't tell Dad."

"Really?" Her mouth spread into a huge smile. "I love you both so much." She pulled me into her arms and then ran over to Liam and hugged him. Her face was glowing with happiness. "Okay, I've got to go. But I'll see you next week. You two be safe." She grabbed her luggage once again and wheeled it out to the elevator, slamming the door shut behind her.

"I'm an asshole." Liam finally looked up at me. "What the hell am I doing?"

"You're trying to protect your sister." For the first time, he was starting to see things differently. It proved he was the man that I'd always saw in him.

"No, I was being my dad." He huffed and shook his head. "You hit it right on the head."

"He is who taught you right from wrong." I walked over and took his hands in mine. I lowered my head and caught his gaze. "But you're waking up and becoming your own person."

"Do you think so?" His eyes locked on mine.

I reached up and touched his cheek with my fingertips. "Of course. You let her leave with your blessing. That counts for something." I stood on my tiptoes and pressed my lips against his.

A low growl emanated from his chest. "You do realize we've got this place to ourselves and it's been close to two weeks since I've been able to touch you? Are you sure you want to be kissing me right now?"

"Most definitely." It felt like forever since he'd touched me. I kissed him again, deepening our kiss.

I don't want to hurt you. He responded to my kiss, and his fingers dug into my sides.

Maybe I want you to. I wrapped my arms around his waist and slipped my fingers along his waistline.

Even if you wanted me to, I couldn't. His hands slid down my waist, all the way to my ass. He grabbed me and pulled me flush against his hardness. *I love you too much.*

As long as I don't raise my arm above my shoulder, I'm

good. I unbuttoned his khakis, reaching further down until I felt him.

Dammit. He reached down to pick me up in his arms before heading down the hallway and into my bedroom. He shut the door and locked it. "In case she forgot something." He laid me on the bed and unzipped his pants, removing them as well as his boxers.

I took a second to enjoy the view before he climbed over me. He began unbuttoning my shirt as his lips found mine once more. His kisses were making me dizzy. He reached underneath me and unfastened my bra, lifting me up to remove both items from my body. "Damn, you're so beautiful."

He kissed his way down my neck and stopped at my breasts, focusing on them. His teeth and tongue working their magic along my body. His hands worked gently, removing my jeans and panties until only his shirt was between us.

"Can you take off your shirt?" I hated to ask since I loved unwrapping him, but my shoulder would scream in pain, and then he wouldn't go any further. I didn't want him to stop.

"Yeah." He sat up and removed his shirt, revealing his large, sculpted muscles underneath.

I reached out and ran my fingers over them as he lowered himself back over me.

His lips met mine again and his hand traveled down-ward, hitting just the right spot. Within moments, my breathing increased as the friction started to build. "It's been so long."

"Damn right it has." His mouth went back to my breasts, and the sensations inside me began magnifying.

"It's my turn." I pushed him over and climbed on top.

He scooted toward the head of the bed and propped himself up as his lips met mine again.

I started to move slow, enjoying him inside me. It wasn't long though before we both began breathing fast.

He moaned as I increased the speed, bringing us both closer to our climax. He began moving with me, and within seconds, we both released together.

I love you. His words were a whisper in my mind as I collapsed against his body. He turned so I could lie on my uninjured side and wrapped his arms around me.

"I'm going to take the other two to the airport. I'll tell them you had to do something and will meet us there." Evan stood at the door to Liam's bedroom, looking at both of us.

It was six in the morning, Liam and I were moving slow. After our round at my dorm, we came back here for a few more before we finally fell asleep only a few hours ago.

"That's the best idea." Liam zipped up his bag and laid it next to mine. "We need to be pretty much taking off before they see her; otherwise, Simon may be tempted to call his dad."

"It's not like they'd given you any choice." Evan frowned. "They'd kidnapped her in broad daylight. With you gone, they could just bust into the dorm and take her from there."

I hadn't even considered that before now, but he was right. Most everyone had gone home for the holiday. If they knew there was a chance of me staying at the dorms alone, they could take me effortlessly.

"Don't freak her out," Liam warned as he reached over and took my hand.

"I'm not trying to, but she needs to get a grasp on whom she's up against." Evan shook his head. "We all need to be vigilant. Our parents aren't exactly who we thought they were."

"No, he's right." I gave Liam a small smile. "I need to start thinking about things like that."

"See, she gets it." Evan took a step back. "Be there in thirty. Our plane leaves at six forty-five." He turned around, and within seconds, the front door opened and shut.

"Do you really think they'll handle it well?" Who was I kidding? Simon was going to lose his shit.

"It'll be fine. Otherwise, we leave." He shrugged his shoulders as if it wasn't a huge deal. "Let's go find something to eat and have you take some more Advil before we leave."

My stomach growled in response. "I guess we have burned a lot of calories."

"I'd be up for losing some more." He winked at me.

My body warmed at the thought.

"Tonight when we're settled in our hotel room." He leaned over and kissed my swollen lips. "Right now, getting you food and medicine is more important."

"Nah." I grinned at him and kissed his lips once more.

"I wouldn't be a good mate if I didn't take care of you." He kissed my cheek and grabbed both his luggage and mine.

I couldn't hide my laugh.

"What?" He arched an eyebrow.

"You have two bags compared to my one." I had enjoyed watching him pack. He couldn't decide what to take, so he started throwing everything in them.

"You have two." He pointed to my backpack that I was bringing as a carry-on.

"Yup. You got me there." I tried to keep my smile hidden, but he caught sight of it.

"Let's go eat." He shook his head and carried our bags out into the living room.

It wasn't long before we'd eaten, I'd taken my medicine, and we were heading to the airport. As we pulled into the parking lot, I couldn't help but feel anxious. I took a deep breath and climbed out of the car while Liam grabbed our bags from his trunk. As I waited, I put my backpack on.

When he headed over to me, there was a smile playing at the corners of his lips. "Where are you going?"

I pointed to the larger building of the small airport. "Right there, where they keep the planes."

"The private jets are kept over there." He motioned to the smaller one to the left.

"Oh, right." It made sense that they wouldn't take a commercial flight. "Okay."

We made our way through the building and headed to a small jet that had a stairwell built into the open door. An older woman dressed as a flight attendant stood at the door. "Mr. Hale, we were getting worried. Here, let me take care of your bags." Her brown eyes landed on me, and her eyebrows raised. "Are you bringing a friend?"

"I'll take care of the luggage, and no, this is my mate, Mia." He nodded at her as he carried the three bags up the stairs.

She startled, shaking her composure, but then smiled at me. "Go on. I'll close the door behind you." The woman took a step closer to me, and her musky scent alerted me to the fact that she was a wolf as well.

"Thank you." I climbed up the stairs to find Liam putting our bags in a storage area in the front of the plane.

"It's about damn time that you got here." Simon's obnoxious voice was like nails on a chalkboard. "I thought you might bail and stay back with your lame-ass mate."

I turned the corner and locked eyes with him. "No, the lame-ass mate is here and will be part of your tour."

"What the fuck? I should've known something was up when you didn't ride with us." Simon glanced at Liam and shook his head. "She can't go on this." He looked at Micah and Evan. "Tell him."

"Actually, I helped him, so I'm good with it." Evan shrugged as he walked past the first recliner and then a couch, to the chair on the other side, and sat.

"Dude, she saved my life. I'm fine with her being here." Micah moved and sat on the first chair directly across from Evan.

I couldn't believe how nice this aircraft was. The colors were from Wolf Moon Academy. The leather couch and recliners were silver and the carpet was blood-red. A dark cherry coffee table sat in the center just like it was a living room back home.

Past those chairs was another set of recliners sitting across from one another. There was even a desk next to it like it was a working area.

"Has everyone here lost their damn mind?" Simon glanced from one heir to the other until his eyes landed back on me. "You're ruining everything. If they see her with us, they're going to ask questions. Our dads will find out."

"Let me make it clear. She goes or I leave." Liam got in Simon's face and narrowed his eyes. "I'm tired of your shit and am looking for any excuse to beat your ass after what you did to Max."

"To who?" Simon's brow furrowed.

"My brother," I said the words loud and slow just to make sure the idiot understood me.

"Oh, that was so two or three weeks ago." Simon laughed. "You can't still be upset over that."

"Actually, she can be, and dammit, I am too. You purposely hurt her in the worst way, and you damn well know it. So what's it going to be, Simon?" Liam crossed his arms. "Are you going to stand down and let this plane take off like it should, or are you going to call your father? If it's the latter, Mia and I will march off this plane and go back home."

Simon growled as he glared at me. "Forget this shit."

He pulled out his phone, but right before he could hit send, Liam rushed him. He twisted Simon's arm, causing him to drop his phone.

"What the hell, man?" Simon spun around, shoving Liam off him with another hand. "That's not fucking cool." He reached for his phone.

Before he could get it, Evan wrapped an arm around his neck, putting him in a chokehold.

"Dude, it's one thing to be supportive of her, but you're hurting one of our own." Micah's eyes flickered back and forth from Simon to Evan.

"You weren't worth the bullet she took for you," Liam growled as he shoved Micah hard.

"Whoa, wait." Micah ran his hands through his short, dark hair. "I'm fine with her coming. I just think everyone is going too far."

I had to agree with that, but the more I was around Simon, the more unstable I realized he truly was. He had no remorse for what he did to my brother. To him, it was just a normal daily occurrence.

"I don't think we've gone far enough." Liam arched an eyebrow. "Unfortunately, there are sides now, and you'd better figure out which one you're on. Being in the middle just aggravates him ..." Liam said as he pointed at Simon, "further."

Evan tightened his grip around Simon's neck. "Are you going to be a dumbass or finally agree?"

Simon's face was turning a shade pale as he struggled to breathe. He waited a few more seconds before he nodded his head.

"Good." Evan released him and snatched the phone off the ground. "Now, I'm taking your cell phone. We don't need you texting your father."

He crumpled on the floor and took in a few deep breaths. His hate-filled eyes looked up and locked on me. "Fine, but the first mistake she makes, she's gone."

"That's fine." Liam nodded his head. "If she makes a mistake, she and I will head home without arguing."

Simon huffed and glared at Liam. "I hope she's worth it." He spun on his heel and headed to the seats in the back.

I wasn't sure if I should be relieved or more worried. He was crazy, and I never knew what to expect from him. I knew one thing for sure... this trip wasn't going to be boring.

CHAPTER TWELVE

The entire plane ride, Liam and I sat on the couch beside each other with Micah and Evan sitting on the recliners next to us. Simon refused to join us and stayed in the back, watching some show.

Where are we going? I just realized I had no clue how many stops we were making and what we were going to do on each of them. I laid my head on Liam's shoulder.

First stop is New York, so Evan will be front and center. Liam kissed the top of my head. *We'll meet with the regional alpha there and take a tour of some of the shifter owned businesses.*

"Wait... Isn't that Robyn girl the daughter of the eastern regional alpha?" I disliked that girl with a flaming passion. Her quickly agreeing to soak my clothes in skunk smell in an attempt to get close to the heirs had left me with a bitter taste in my mouth. Her constant snide remarks didn't make it any better either.

"If you think she's bad, wait until you meet her father." Evan shook his head and rolled his eyes. "There is a reason why my dad made me tough."

"Fat lot of good it did you," Simon said as he glanced from the television. "You've sided with Liam over a girl that's a nobody. If that doesn't show you're weak, I don't know what else will. You three are making a huge mistake letting her tag along."

"Other than my dad only being a pack alpha, what is your problem with me?" I hated the tension that was so thick in the cabin. It felt as if it was suffocating me.

"Oh, you think there is only one?" Simon's deep chuckle sounded crazed. "I've got a whole fucking list."

"Then name them." I had to at least make sure I understood why he hated me so much.

"The first one is your lack of raising and respect." Simon jumped to his feet and stood in front of me. "You should have never talked to us like that at the party. You are nothing, just a waste of air."

Liam growled in warning.

I asked him. Let him have his say. If he was trying to hurt me, it wouldn't happen, but I had to understand how his mind worked. "And two?" I stared him in the eyes, daring him to continue.

"You're weak." He spat the words at me. "You're too close to your friends and family and care too damn much about nearly everything and everyone. You aren't built for the world we," he said as he pointed to the four heirs, "live in. If you'd been smart that day at the abandoned repair shop, you'd have let that bullet hit Micah."

"Are you being serious right now?" Micah's eyes widened, and he shook his head. "You would have let me die?"

He shrugged. "One less heir and more power for the remaining three."

"Wow, that's cold, man. You do realize we couldn't take

over his council seat, right?" Liam arched an eyebrow. "The council itself almost didn't survive after Brent died. Taking it down to three would cause civil unrest. Now that I see what your real motive is, I won't forget it."

"Brent?" Simon shook his head and frowned. "You're putting a name to the overseer now, which means she's fucking with your mind. You can't personalize him. He was a casualty of war."

"War?" This couldn't be real. "He was a council member. How in the hell does that make sense?"

"And that brings me to the third point. You don't realize how things work." Simon waved his hand around to the three other heirs. "We're always at war with one another. Strong alphas always compete, constantly trying to take over the next level. It's in our blood."

"No, it's not." I couldn't believe his twisted view of reality. "When you let your animal part take over more than it should, that's when you become that way. Strong leaders want to take care of the ones below them. They aren't solely focused on coming out on top."

"This proves my point further. To be a good leader, you should be revered and feared." Simon held his hands out to his sides. "The four of us were like fucking gods until you interfered."

"Gods? That's how you think the packs view you?" For the first time, I realized what his problem was. He was scared and didn't want to get hurt. It was easier to push everyone away and justify it with his strength than to admit his own fear. "I hate to tell you this, but that's not it at all. They view you as leaders, not gods. And for the last few years, they've been questioning everything to see if you're even listening to them anymore."

"We don't have to listen; we know what's right." Simon

sneered at me. "And these three idiots feel the same way. You've just managed to mess with their heads. You're nothing but a manipulative bitch."

"That's enough." Liam's voice was cold, and his body tensed. "Say one more bad thing about her and I'll make something bad happen to you."

My heart warmed at how he was standing up for me. It was amazing how our relationship had changed everything so quickly. Once he'd stopped fighting our bond, he was all in.

"Liam," Simon started, but Liam cut him off.

"For the first time in our entire lives, we have someone with us who isn't trying to get something out of us. Do you really think Evan would've warmed to her if that wasn't true? He didn't like anyone before her and was probably on the same page as you." Liam stood and faced him head-on. "She risked her life for Micah, which is something you even admitted that you would never do. Why the hell doesn't she deserve our loyalty?"

"She's doing it all to mess with us." Simon lifted both hands in front of him. "And your judgment is clouded because fate is trying to screw you over."

"Yes, I got shot just to mess with you all." He was insane. "It hurt like a bitch, and I couldn't breathe without excruciating pain, all so I can fuck with every one of your heads." At this point, I gave up. "Forget I asked for your reasons. I'm not interested in them anymore."

"Honestly, I hate that it's come to this, but like you said, the old us were only out for ourselves." Liam's blue eyes darkened, and he shook his head. "You keep it up, and you're going to be left all alone." Liam sat back next to me and pulled me into his lap.

"I can't be alone. We're in this together." Simon's face

fell, and he placed a hand on his chest. "The four of us always have to stay together for our future. That's the whole point of this trip."

"Just because we have to see each other doesn't mean we're on the same side." Evan arched an eyebrow and cut his eyes at him. "It would be good to remember that."

The flight attendant appeared from the front of the cabin. "We're beginning to descend, so please take your seats. We'll be on the ground in twenty minutes."

I took a deep breath. I had to get my nerves together, or New York could be more of a train wreck than the flight here.

THE EAST WAS ACTUALLY what humans called the northeast today. It was everything from Pennsylvania and New Jersey up.

Since New York was part of the eastern territory, Evan took lead as we exited the plane. Liam and Micah were on either side of me as we followed directly behind Evan. Simon pouted as he followed in the very back.

As soon as we entered the building, we saw two large men who distinctly smelled of wolves. The taller and larger man had red hair and muddy brown eyes. He had to be Robyn's father. He puffed his chest out as our group of five approached him. He was only a couple of inches taller than me, and he wore a suit that hugged his entire body, including his large belly.

The city alpha was almost the same size as the other man, but his presence wasn't quite as commanding. He was a little more slender, but his black suit was also a little more forgiving. He was about my height but balding.

When his yellow eyes met my own, a shiver ran down my spine.

"Mr. Lyndon and Mr. Grover." Evan gave a small, tight smile. "Thanks for meeting us here. You, of course, didn't have to."

"We want to welcome the future members of the council here personally." Mr. Grover lifted his head and grinned. "After all, my dear, sweet Robyn is going to the academy this year. Of course, you all know she talks about how you hang out with her from time to time."

"Oh, does she now?" Simon snickered from behind.

"What is that supposed to mean?" Mr. Grover's smile changed to a scowl.

In this exact moment, he could be a dead ringer for his daughter. That scowl was the constant expression she had on her face.

"Ignore him. Something happened on the plane that has him out of sorts." Liam stepped forward, taking hold of the situation. "I'm Liam, the heir to the northern seat."

"It's a huge honor to meet you." The city alpha stepped in front of Mr. Grover. "I'm Mr. Lyndon, and I'm the one who runs this city with the support of Mr. Grover."

Liam glanced at Evan.

Evan nodded in return and took a step back.

"This is Micah, who is the heir of the south, and Simon, who is the western heir." Liam stepped forward, handling the introductions. *Evan hates talking and dealing with politics.*

Ah, so you were asking for permission to take over? That's what that whole exchange between them was about.

Of course. This is his territory. Liam stepped beside me and held my hand.

You do realize that all four of you are responsible for not only your territory but each other's, right? It reminded me of how Professor Johnson had talked about the initial Blood Council. *Yes, you have your own area you represent, but when you make decisions, it should be for the good of all of the people.*

"And who might this pretty young lady be?" Mr. Lyndon once again locked his gaze on me, and his eyes traveled to Liam's and my joined hands.

"'This is my mate, Mia." Liam nodded toward me.

Simon shook his head and openly cringed at those words.

"I didn't realize one of the heirs had already chosen." Mr. Lyndon leered as he stepped in my direction.

"We're fated mates." Liam stepped slightly in front of me, effectively cutting the city alpha off. "Are we ready to go?"

"Uh... yes." Mr. Grover appeared to have recovered as he motioned for us to head in the direction of the front of the building. "We ordered a limo and figured we could take you to lunch at Mr. Lyndon's restaurant so we can discuss business. We also have some tickets for a show for you tonight. We thought you might want to get settled and have a nice night before leaving in the morning."

"Great." Evan headed toward the door at a near sprint.

The rest of us followed behind, keeping our thoughts to ourselves.

When we reached the door, Mr. Grover rushed to catch up with Evan. The automatic doors opened, and Mr. Grover pointed at the only limousine in front like we couldn't have figured it out.

The valet opened the doors, and Evan was the first to get in. Liam tugged on my arm, indicating that I get in right behind the eastern alphas, so I followed suit with Liam climbing in after me.

Soon, the heirs were all sitting on one side of the car while the two eastern alphas sat in the shorter seat opposite, facing us.

"I'm so glad you decided to visit us. I heard that we're your first stop. This city is amazing, and we've done so much for our people." Mr. Lyndon grinned as he pointed out the window. "We have restaurants here. Some of our people are even in the Broadway shows while some are teachers, helping influence the minds of both shifters and human children."

"This is similar to the way it is in Boston and other areas as well, but of course, nothing is quite like New York." Mr. Grover leaned into us like he was letting us in on a very well-kept secret.

Wow, they are full of shit. For them to be trying this hard, it made me wonder what in the hell they were covering up.

A huge grin spread across Liam's face before he was able to school it back into a neutral expression. *I love how you call things as you see them.*

Good, because that will never change. I stopped listening to the two idiots babble on about whatever great things they were doing. All I heard were a few words repeated over and over again; best, amazing, world-changing, and influencing. *When someone tries to sell you a used car, they only tell you the good things and not the bad. So what are they hiding?*

You think they're up to something? Liam squeezed my hand and glanced out the window.

It's New York City. My eyes took in the sights as we drove by. The roads were packed, and so were the sidewalks. Everyone, from people wearing suits to homeless people, walked within the hordes. *It's the perfect city to hide things that others would want to keep buried.*

Well, I guess we're about to find out. Liam glanced over at Micah.

The southern heir had a blank look on his face, but he seemed to be trying to pay attention.

Soon, the car began slowing down, and we pulled up to a restaurant that was right across from Central Park.

The driver jumped from the car to open the door so all of us could climb out. As we moved into the restaurant, Mr. Lyndon headed to the hostess' stand. As soon as the hostess saw him, she immediately had menus out and ready.

I paused a second to take in the restaurant. It was an older building with dark cherry wood throughout, even on the walls. There was a large bar stationed at the left side with hundreds of bottles of wine, liquor, and beers filling every cabinet. Glasses of all types hung from underneath the cabinet, leaving the counters empty and ready to be used.

Come on. Liam tugged on my hand as we followed the city alpha through the restaurant, passing a few tables strategically scattered throughout the space, toward the back. We entered a private area with a table already set up for six.

"Oh, we need one more chair immediately." Mr. Lyndon turned to Liam and me. "We didn't know there would be five of you, so please be patient while she gets another chair for your mate."

"She shouldn't be here." Simon's whisper was low enough so the alphas couldn't hear but Liam and I could.

Liam turned his head and gave him a warning.

Simon lifted both hands in the air as if in surrender.

I want you to sit between Evan and me. Liam took the lead and placed me in the middle of one side. We moved like clockwork, Evan sitting immediately on one side of me while Liam sat on the other. Micah sat across from Liam, and Simon sat directly in front of me. Soon, the hostess appeared, and the city alpha wound up sitting at the end of the table between Evan and Mr. Grover.

Within minutes, we had our drinks and food ordered; that was when they decided to begin talking business.

"We need more funds so we can attract more humans to our businesses." Mr. Lyndon leaned forward, making sure he met with every one of the heirs' eyes, but he avoided mine like the plague. "Yes, we have to keep our identity a secret, but dammit, the more they depend on us, the better. You never know what the future will bring."

"That's what all the large eastern cities need. My region has the most people in it despite its small size. That means we have to monopolize the markets in other creative ways. Like, for instance, the show you'll see tonight; it's located at a place we could buy out. Think of the diversity it would bring to our overall portfolio."

I hate to do this, but I'm going to run to the bathroom. I really should have stayed and listened, but it didn't interest me. These people weren't talking about how their packs were doing, only how to make each one of them richer.

Do I need to come with you? Liam's eyes met mine.

No, I'm fine. I'll let you know if I fall into the toilet and need help. He was a little too overprotective sometimes, but I couldn't blame him.

Fine. His warm chuckle sounded in my head.

"Excuse me, gentlemen, but where can I find the ladies' room?" I glanced at the two alphas, not sure which one would respond.

"Sure, you can use the staff bathroom. It's in the back corner." Mr. Lyndon pointed back toward the direction we'd entered. "To the right. You can't miss it."

"Okay, thanks." I turned on my heel, desperate to get out of the room for a second. As I followed his instructions, I heard someone crying. I hurried toward the noise, which took me straight to where he had directed.

"I have to figure out something. She's sick. She can't live in those conditions." A girl's voice broke in pain.

"You know there isn't a damn thing we can do." Another voice sounded upset but devoid of hope. "All of us that don't provide them any value have to live there. There are no exceptions. You know they'd put all of us out on our asses if we tried anything. We're stuck."

"She's going to die. She's barely moving; she's so still that I find rats and their feces all over her." The girl broke down again. "I can't lose her."

The older woman's tone hardened. "Yes, she's a shifter, but even we have to die at some point. You need to grow up and realize that."

My heart sank into my stomach. I opened the door to find a young woman with tears pouring down her cheeks, talking with a woman who had to be in her fifties. The girl wiped her tears away from her chocolate-colored eyes, and the older one stiffened, blowing out a breath.

"I'm sorry to interrupt. I was told to find the bathrooms here." I looked down the small hall that led to two stalls.

"Oh, we were done here." The older one glared at the younger girl as she grabbed a paper towel and handed it to her. "She came in with the alphas and the heirs."

The younger girl licked her lips. "We'll get out of your way."

"Wait." I didn't want them to go.

They both flinched at my command.

"If we wanted to come by and check on your pack tonight, where would we go?"

The girl spun around with what could only have been hope in her eyes. "We live off Fulton Street."

"Shush. Nothing good can come of this." The older one met my gaze, and something akin to hate filled her eyes. "Just leave us alone, and stop playing with our lives. Don't give us hope when all you elite people only take from us." The older woman grabbed the younger one's arm. "You've done enough. We need to go."

As the door shut behind them, my heart felt heavy. There was no way in hell I was going to some play tonight when our people were struggling. It was time to see what really went on when the regional and city alphas weren't around to watch and direct our every move.

CHAPTER THIRTEEN

As I stepped out of the bathroom, my mind replayed the conversation I'd overheard. Something didn't seem right, but I couldn't quite put my finger on it. Obviously, the place they lived was a dump, but why couldn't they move? And why segregate them from humans? It made no sense.

Someone cleared their throat, causing me to look in their direction.

Mr. Grover stood about five feet away from me, leaning against the dark cherry wooden wall. His muddy eyes turned dark as he glowered at me. Robyn had definitely learned that particular look from him.

I moved to walk past him, but he grabbed my arm a little too hard, yanking me back toward him.

"I was under the impression that my daughter was dating the northern heir." His face turned into a sneer. "So what a surprise to find him bring not only a girl but his fated mate with him."

Of course, he was going to try to bully and intimidate me. The more elite people I met, the more unworthy they became in my eyes. "Well, maybe you misunderstood her. Liam never dated her."

I moved to pull my arm out of his grip, but he dug his fingers in deeper.

"There was no misunderstanding. How the fuck did someone like you catch his eye? From what she told me, your dad is just a pack alpha, and Liam got her to put you in your place." He frowned, and his nose wrinkled in disgust. "You aren't worthy of him. You're probably just a plaything."

"You know as well as I do that he's claimed me." Every shifter could smell when someone was claimed. It became two distinct scents combined into one.

"But there are ways to handle that." His eyes flashed with something akin to hunger. "All it takes is one accident."

I almost alerted Liam of what was happening, but this was something I had to do on my own. The more it looked like he was protecting me, the worse it would be. I needed to start relying on my own wolf to handle these situations. "I'd be careful who you threaten."

"What can someone like you do?" He chuckled like it was the funniest thing he'd ever heard. "Tell the heir on me? He won't believe you."

"Why is that?" I needed to understand how all these jackasses really thought.

"I'm a strong alpha male. Everyone weak gets intimidated by me." He waved his other hand in the air. "It was just a misguided, weak wolf's misunderstanding of the entire situation."

Wow, and I thought it wouldn't get uglier. "I'm not leaving Liam if that's what you're getting at. And if you feel brave enough to try to do something to me, bring it on." I yanked my arm away from his grasp and allowed my wolf to bleed through. "We're done here."

His eyes widened at what they found, but I turned on my heel and headed back to the table. I needed to tell Liam as soon as we were done here what had gone down.

THE REST of the dinner passed in a blur, and I still couldn't get over Mr. Grover's nerve as we walked into our hotel room in the Baccarat Hotel. My mouth dropped open at the white modern feel of the room that had to cost a small fortune. The sheets and couch were solid white and there was a small, straight-line coffee table in the center. Our bags had already been delivered and were sitting next to the table.

"Do you think we should have stayed with the others? It probably would've been less expensive." The other three heirs got a suite that they were sharing. Liam had demanded that we have our own room.

"Hell, no." His jaw clenched as he glared at the door. "I don't trust that psychopath."

"I take it you mean Simon." That was a dead-on analysis.

"He's always been the crazier one out of the four of us, but it didn't hit until now how out of his mind he truly is." Liam pulled me into his arms. "He can't be trusted at all."

"I don't think it's entirely his fault." For him to act like that, something tragic had to have happened.

"You're too forgiving." He pushed a piece of my hair behind my ear. "But we're still safer here away from them."

That, I couldn't disagree with. "So about tonight..." I hadn't told him yet what I'd overheard since I didn't want to interfere with the meeting they were having. If you could even call it that; it was only about how they needed more money to make money. Not once did they mention the poor conditions in which some of the packs were living.

"Are you excited about seeing the play? I think it's Phantom of the Opera." A small grin spread across his face.

"I don't think we should go." I hated saying it. I'd always wanted to go watch an opera.

"Why not?" His forehead creased as he tilted his head at me.

I filled him in on what I had overheard at the restaurant. "I think we need to go check it out."

"I'm sure they'd let us know if they were..." His words trailed off, and he took in a deep breath. "No, they wouldn't let us know, would they?"

"Nope." It was like watching him sift through sand as a part of him woke up that he'd never even known was dormant. "All they talked about was ways to make themselves and all of you more money."

"Dammit." He leaned his forehead against mine. "I've never noticed that stuff before, but you're right."

"So are you okay with my plan?"

"Yeah, you're right. We need to go check it out." He took in a deep breath and let it out. "Let me text Evan so he's not waiting for us."

I glanced at the clock and couldn't believe how late it was. It was almost six in the evening. That meeting had felt like it took forever for a damn good reason.

He pulled his phone from his pocket and typed a message. "Are you ready to go?"

The sooner we got there, the better. "Yeah."

As we walked out the door, the heirs' room opened with the three of them in the doorway.

"What are you doing?" Liam's body tensed as if he was preparing for a fight.

"We want to go with you." Micah shrugged his shoulder as he glanced from me back to Liam. "It's not like I really wanted to go watch that show anyway."

"Are you sure you want to do this?" Liam's eyes landed on Evan. "If we do find something, it'll be hardest for you to turn your back on it."

I squeezed Liam's hand. He was trying to be a friend to Evan, but this was something we all needed to see. I hadn't wanted to force them to go, but if they were willing, we needed to take them up on their offer.

"Yeah, I'm sure." Evan nodded his head and stepped into the hallway with us.

"I've got a limo downstairs, waiting on us." Micah stepped beside Evan.

"Wait. No." Were they crazy? "You're expecting us to roll up to a place that has horrible living conditions in a fucking limo?"

They all blinked as they processed what I said.

"No, we can take a taxi just like anyone else." I'd feel like an asshole doing that.

"For the record, I think this is all bullshit and we should just go to the show or to a bar to find a quick lay." Simon's cold frown landed on me. "But of course, none of you listen to anyone ... but her now."

"Will you stop with the bullshit?" Liam's growl was way too loud for a hotel hallway. He was beginning to lose control. "I'm so tired of your mouth. None of us give a damn about what you think anymore."

Simon's amber eyes began to glow.

"You two knock it off." We didn't need them shifting and fighting right here in the hallway. "Let's go. Simon, you don't have to go if you don't want to." I turned on my heel and headed toward the elevator.

Hey, he was being an asshole. Liam caught up to me, his jaw still clenched.

And we're out here where humans could see and hear us. I don't think Simon takes any of that into account when he starts things with you, and I think he provokes you in public on purpose. I hit the elevator door, and the five of us piled inside.

The ride down was quiet, and when we walked out onto the sidewalk, Liam hailed two cabs.

He and I got in one, and the remaining three got in the other. We gave them the road and the description of the apartment building, and then we were on our way.

It took nearly twenty minutes to get there with all of the traffic. When we pulled up to the building, I couldn't believe my eyes. It was a brick building, but some windows were busted out or cracked. I climbed out of the car, followed by Liam. We both stood there and waited for the others.

Shifters definitely live here. Liam took my hand and glanced over his shoulder at the other three heirs as they got out of their cab.

I have a feeling it's going to be even worse inside. I headed to the front door.

Simon hissed behind me. "Why is everyone okay with her taking the lead?" He pushed Evan in the shoulder. "That should be you."

"Shut up." Evan glared at Simon. "Touch me one more time, and see what happens."

"Just come on, man." Micah grabbed Simon's arm and

pulled him after me. "It's best if you keep that damn mouth of yours closed."

Not even bothering to pay attention to his incessant griping, I pulled at the main door, expecting it to be locked, but it swung open. "That's not very safe." Then, the scent of feces and urine hit my nose, causing me to gag.

Liam stepped into the place, and I followed directly after him with the other three coming in behind us. There was a set of stairs to the right where the railing hung down, not even connecting to the steps. Liam bypassed it, going straight to the end where a long hallway stretched off to the right and left. There were water stains streaked down the walls and ceiling, and a rat scurried by on the dingy, brown carpet.

It sounded like a television was on in one of the rooms to the right, so Liam turned in that direction.

He lifted his hand and knocked on the door.

The television stopped, and the sound of footsteps led to the door. "Who is it?" The voice cracked with age.

"It's the heirs to the council." Liam's voice was scratchy, and he cleared his throat.

"Is this some kind of joke?" The door opened, revealing a man who was Liam's height but was hunched over and so thin that skin hung from his skeleton. His almost white eyes widened. "Holy shit." He took in Liam, then me, and then the three huge men behind me.

A door a few apartments down swung open to reveal a younger woman—or at least, I thought she was—who glanced down the hall at us. Her expression seemed young, but her hair was limp, her eyes sunken, and her posture was hunched.

"Look, don't you think we've paid enough for it?" The older man stumbled back with fear shining in his eyes.

"What do you mean?" Liam said his words slowly as surprise filtered through our bond.

"Don't act like you don't know. Why else would you be here?" His lower lip quivered. "We now live in a dump where it hurts to breathe. Isn't that penance enough?"

"Have you told anyone about the conditions you live in?" Something had to be amiss, or at least, I hoped. However, after what I had heard earlier, I doubted it. "Like Mr. Lyndon or Mr. Grover?"

The old man started cackling. "Who the hell do you think did this to us? Hell, Mr. Lyndon is our landlord."

"There has to be a reason for this." Evan's face was a mask of indifference.

I'd learned that his neutral expression was used when he felt too many emotions. It made him appear cold, but it was actually when he cared the most.

"Oh, there is." The old man paused and took us all in. "You really are clueless, aren't you? Your dad didn't tell you?"

"Tell us what?" Micah took a step toward the old man so he could look inside his apartment.

"We heard that The Blood Council was giving our city more money, so we had asked for help with the cost of living. It's hard to survive here and blend in with the humans. Mr. Grover and Mr. Lyndon ignored our requests, so I went straight to the top. After all, I'm their pack alpha. One week later, we got an answer. One we had thought was a blessing."

This wasn't going in a good direction. I glanced around and saw several people now leaning out their doors, watching us. They all looked greasy and unkempt like they didn't even have running water.

"They said they bought us an apartment building so our

whole pack could live together and we would only have to pay a thousand a month each. Here, that's cheap, so we jumped at the opportunity. We have to live in packs here and only where the city alpha will allow us. When we rolled up here, we thought, surely, they were going to remodel. After ten years, we gave up hope. It's actually gotten worse instead of better."

"How so?" Evan's voice was deep.

"Well, we don't have clean water any longer. Between the roaches and mice, it's hard to sleep here even in animal form." He shook his head. "Since we caused so many problems, we all could only get low paying jobs cleaning up after the elites of the city. We struggle to feed ourselves, and we can't go out in wolf form often because it's the city."

"I'm sure you all deserved it." Simon sneered at the older man. "Let's go before we start smelling like this place."

"Shut the fuck up, Simon." Micah's tone was harsh, which was rare for him. He usually didn't talk to any of the heirs that way.

"Well, if we did, there are several others in similar situations. Only a handful of packs here live in good conditions. The only thing we can be thankful for is a roof over our heads, but some days, I think it might be better to live as our animals outside."

"Why don't you move to another city then?" There had to be some other reason that kept them here that I didn't know.

"Because in my region, you have to get approval to move." Evan shook his head and took in a deep breath before wincing. "I can honestly say I had no idea this was happening."

"But will you make changes when you come into power?" The older man's eyes barely glowed.

He was weak, but his pack wasn't worth taking over. No one person would choose to live here.

A baby screamed at the end of the hall where a lady was standing. She rocked the little angel in her arms, but the baby kept wailing louder.

My eyes landed on the scene, and I took a few steps down the hall. I approached the woman slowly since she looked so frightened. "Is she okay?" I finally could see the baby clearly, and she was bone thin as well.

"She's just hungry." The mom's eyes filled with tears. "I can't breastfeed her because we don't have enough to eat ... and we get formula as often as we can."

My heart broke. These people might as well be home-less, and yet they still paid a monthly rate to live this way. *We need to do something. These people can't starve.*

We'll order them some pizzas, and I'll get some groceries delivered too. Liam's eyes met mine. *It'll have to do until we can go home and make a change.*

SIMON AND MICAH HAD LEFT, but Evan, Liam, and I helped deliver groceries to each apartment in the building. We made sure each household with children got larger supplies of whatever they needed.

We were pretty sure we had found the person that the young lady had been so upset about in the restaurant's bath-room. When we entered her room, an older lady was weak and lying on the ground. The alpha had told us about how she'd stepped on a nail or something and within the next few days, she couldn't open her mouth. That was two weeks ago, and she hadn't been able to eat or drink since then. She looked as if she was already at death's door.

With Evan being pre-med, he had known it was tetanus immediately and cleaned the wound on her foot, which still hadn't healed from the toxins. He explained that even though we were shifters, there were certain bacteria that could even take us down. Had she been human, she wouldn't have lasted this long. He called a family friend who dropped antibiotics off while we were still there.

As we headed to leave the place for the night, the older man rushed toward us before we walked out the door.

"I want to say thank you." Tears filled his pale eyes, and he took a deep breath. "We haven't had someone take care of us like this in such a long time. I hope you're able to make the changes needed when you come into power, and remember what The Blood Council is meant to stand for."

Ignoring his smell, I pulled him into my arms and hugged him. "We won't forget." And I meant every word.

CHAPTER FOURTEEN

The night's events had taken a toll on all of us. The ride back to the hotel had been quiet, and as soon as we got into the hotel room, I took a long, hot shower.

My heart was still broken over what we had seen. Yes, we bought them food, treated the ones who needed medicine, and even scheduled a pest control company to handle the rats and roaches. Still, it didn't seem like nearly enough. And the fact that the alpha had alluded to other packs being treated the same way made me want to vomit.

It made me feel horrible for staying in such a nice place. Even the shower was nicer than what I had back home. The white marble tile and rain faucet almost felt sinful to enjoy.

"Are you okay?" Liam's voice was raspy as he slid open the shower door and joined me under the spray.

My eyes soaked up his naked form. His chest muscular, and his strong arms wrapped around my waist, pulling me into him.

"I can't get over what we saw tonight." I had expected it to be bad, but that had been so much worse than what I could have ever imagined. "I don't understand how they could do that to their own people."

"I'm shocked too." His hand ran through my wet hair. "But because of you, we're seeing what's going on, and within the next year, we'll be on the council and can fix everything."

"The next year?" I knew it was coming up soon, but it was faster than I had expected. "When you graduate?"

"Yeah, but don't worry. You'll be able to step into the Overseer role at the same time we ascend. I'll make sure it happens." He lowered his lips onto mine.

Some of my worries melted away as my body warmed to his touch. *What are you and the others graduating in? I know Evan is pre-med, but it's strange that I have no clue about your major.* The mate bond was unusual in that your soul recognized its other half, but the small details like majors and family life were things you had to learn about one another just as humans did.

I'm majoring in Business while Micah is majoring in Economics. He pulled back as his shoulders started shaking. *And Simon is Communications.*

That had to be a joke. *You've got to be kidding me?*

Believe it or not, he can be convincing when it's something he believes in. Liam leaned down and kissed my lips again. *But enough about them. Right now, I want to give my amazing, caring mate some much-needed attention.* His hands slipped between my legs.

As he touched me, everything else seemed to fade away in my mind. His touch was doing wonderful things to my body.

He began trailing kisses down my neck and stopped at my breast. Water coated both of us, but in this moment, it was like it didn't exist. Right now, his touch and lips were making me delirious.

My back was against the cool tile wall as he thrust inside me. With each move, he connected with me more in both physical and emotional form.

He was upset about what he'd seen too, but he knew we could overcome anything.

It was amazing because even though I loved him with every fiber of my being, I managed to still fall in love with him more and more with each passing day. I moaned as his fingers dug into my waist, holding me steady as I wrapped my legs around him.

His lips claimed mine again, and my head grew dizzy. His smell, his touch, and his mouth were the only things that mattered to me at that moment.

It was only a short time later that we both climaxed. His body leaned toward mine as he pulled me against his chest and into his arms.

At that moment, I knew no matter what happened, we'd get through it together.

"So, now we're going to bumblefuck." Simon pouted as he dropped into his usual spot on the airplane, away from the four of us. "After hanging out in that hell hole, I now have to go get dirty in the south."

"You do realize I'm from there, right?" Micah arched a dark eyebrow as he took his usual seat in the recliner where his back was toward him.

"Yeah, and your room is disgusting." Simon leaned back in his chair as he turned on the television. "So if the shoe fits."

"Shut the hell up." Evan rolled his eyes. "And stop trying to piss everyone off."

"If you gave me back my cell phone, I'd be good and distracted." He arched an eyebrow.

"No, we don't trust you." Liam glanced at him as he sat on the couch. "No way in hell you're getting it back until after the trip."

"For all you know, my father could be worried sick about me." Simon's voice dropped a little lower, but it was almost unnoticeable.

"Yeah, right." Micah laughed. "He hasn't texted you once. We've been keeping an eye on it."

Simon's face fell, and he leaned back in his seat.

That hurt his feelings. To be honest, that was something a little unexpected.

He's always tried to keep his dad's attention, but it's fleeting. That's one reason why he acts out at times or goes to such drastic measures to get noticed by his dad. Liam frowned and shrugged. *It's always been that way, but he seems to be handling it better now.*

I didn't think he was, but this wasn't the time to analyze it. "Where are we headed now?" I had no clue what all the stops were other than the main regions. New York City was cool, but one day I hoped to go back under better circumstances. There was a lot of sightseeing I'd wanted to do. Maybe Bree and I could have a girls' trip.

"Atlanta." Micah's golden eyes seemed to shine a little brighter. "Where I grew up half the time. The regional alpha and city alpha will be there just like in New York."

"Apparently, Dad informed me alphas will be at each stop. It's part of the tour to get to know the regional and the city leaders." Liam wrapped an arm around my shoulders against the back of the couch. "Then, we'll do another tour where we visit another large city, and we'll meet the district alpha and that city's alpha as well. Most big-city alphas technically report to a district alpha but usually bypass them the majority of the time. Mainly because of the size and the magnitude of what's going on in their areas. So the regional alpha spends more time with them, and the district alphas spend more time with the smaller cities."

I didn't realize you'd talked to your dad. Mr. Hale must have figured out I was traveling with them.

He called to ask me if it was true you were with us. Liam ran his fingers along my shoulders. *I told him yes. He's pissed but is waiting to lecture me at home.*

We'd have to worry about that later. We had more important things to address. "What I'm hearing you say is that we're only going to hear and see what they want us to? Just like New York." I hated to be so negative, but if New York had taught us anything, it was that there was more going on than we realized. This sort of proved in my mind what my dad had been trying to stand against. Had he known this was coming and tried to protect all the packs from it? Maybe that was why they'd turned against him. He'd wanted to be the leader the packs deserved and not allow it to turn into a position based purely on self-interest.

"I'm sure it was only New York. Our dads couldn't have known." Micah's words seemed unsure at the end. "Right?"

"You're letting that bitch get in your head." Simon stood and glared at me with so much hate. "Of course, they don't know."

"Please sit down, Sir." The flight attendant entered the room. "We're taking off now, and everyone needs to be seated."

"Hey, you don't get to tell me what to do." Simon's eyes glowed as his wolf surged forward.

Evan jumped to his feet and stared down the western heir. "Stop being an overbearing, selfish asshole. Now, shut up before I make you. You know I can do it."

"She's just doing her job, and you're going to make us late," Micah turned to look over his shoulder at Simon. "Stop acting like a girl." Micah winced and glanced at me. "No offense."

"None taken." I probably should have taken offense, but there were a lot of girls who did, in fact, act like that.

Simon refused to budge as he stared back at Evan. That was until Evan took a step in his direction.

"Fine." Simon plopped in the seat and scowled at the television.

It seemed as though he got more aggravated and hostile the longer we were all together.

As we departed the private jet at the Atlanta airport, I was surprised at the size of the building. It was as large as some of the smaller cities' airports combined. We were now in the southern territory, which stretched all the way through Texas, Oklahoma, Arkansas, Kentucky, West Virginia, Delaware, and Maryland downward. So now, it was Micah's turn to shine.

As we entered the building, I was surprised to find that it was filled to the brim with people buzzing around. However, there were two large, towering men off to the side with obvious scents of shifters. Once Micah's gaze landed on them, he nodded and headed in their direction.

One of the men had darker olive skin similar to Micah's, but his face was rigid. His eyes were a pale green, making his presence a little scary. He tugged at the bottom of his gray suit jacket and cleared his throat.

The other man standing next to him had a medium olive skin tone and was only about an inch shorter than the first one. His dark black eyes scanned our group as he placed his hands in the pockets of his charcoal suit.

"Mr. Buckley." Micah shook hands with the taller man and then turned to the other one. "Mr. Haggard. It's nice to see you both again." Then, Micah turned to face our direction. "I'm sure you know the heirs."

"Of course, we do." Mr. Buckley nodded his head before his eyes landed on me. "However, who is she? We had thought only the four of you were visiting."

"She's my mate." Liam stepped forward and took my hand in his. "It's my fault. We're newly mated, and I couldn't fathom leaving her behind."

"I remember those days." Mr. Haggard chuckled. "But I'll be honest, it doesn't get much easier. It's like a piece of you is missing if you're separated for too long."

"I'm Mia." I was not okay with being called Liam's mate the entire time. I had a name too. "And sorry if my unexpected presence has caused a problem."

"We were hoping for your full attention." Mr. Buckley scoffed as his eyes narrowed on me. "Maybe she can go hang out at the hotel room or go shopping while we discuss alpha things."

"Are you insinuating that I can't focus on my duties with her beside me?" Liam straightened his shoulders as he stared the regional leader down. "I find it not only insulting to me but to my mate as well."

"And I'm also concerned about the city and its well-being." I hated how they disregarded me because I was considered only a mate and a woman. It was like they didn't believe women could be alphas despite our history.

"Not a big deal at all." Mr. Haggard lifted a hand. "One call and we can fix it. I thought it might be good to take you to one of the baseball games here. We have, of course, a luxury box."

Naturally. They weren't going to take us anywhere to meet more people.

"Great." Micah shook his head. "It's been a long time since I've been to one of those."

"Then let's go." Mr. Buckley turned and led us out front. Needless to say, there was a limo there, waiting for us.

I had a feeling the next four hours were going to creep by.

THE BOX SEATS were a lot nicer than I expected. Ours was spacious enough for twenty-five people to sit comfortably, but there were only seven of us there. The inside was air-conditioned, and several buffet stations lined the wall behind us, containing standard ballpark foods like hot dogs, nachos, and the like with different kinds of water, Coke, and beer.

A balcony sat directly outside the doorway to watch the game, and there were two adjoined rooms within the box—one where the food was located, which had a table next to it, and then another section with two large couches and chairs surrounding a television. Both were connected to the balcony.

We were all sitting on the balcony, watching the ball-game going on below.

"Did your fathers tell you about the new manufacturing

plant we purchased on the outskirts of town?" Mr. Buckley turned his attention to the heirs.

"No, they didn't." Micah shook his head. "They must have gotten sidetracked."

Yeah, right. They didn't tell them for a reason. I could only imagine the real motive behind it.

"What kind of plant is it?" Liam's hand stiffened in mine.

He had to be wondering the same thing I was.

"It's a chicken processing plant in Gainesville, Georgia." Mr. Haggard grinned and patted Micah's shoulder. "It's generating over five hundred million in revenue this year."

The more I watched Mr. Haggard, the more concerned I got. He was nice and charismatic on the surface. The perfect type of person who could hide something horrible.

"Oh, can we go visit it?" If they were that proud of it, then that would be a reasonable request.

Mr. Haggard laughed as if I'd told a good joke and leaned over Micah so he could see me three seats down. "Oh, dear, no. It's where they kill and process dead chickens. I'm sure you and the heirs don't want to go to a place like that. We only wanted to share the good news. And the best part is we were able to hire all wolf shifters to work there. So not only are we making money for all of us, but we're helping the local packs out."

If they're that proud of it, wouldn't they want us to see it? I hated to be so critical. Yet, after what we saw in New York, I was scared.

I'm thinking the same thing. Liam squeezed my hand.

"I really don't mind going." Liam's eyes landed on Micah, who sat right next to him. "Do you?"

"It might be a good thing for the workers to see the heirs supporting them." Micah shrugged. "So, I'm not opposed."

"Dude, it's a chicken processing factory. Do we really want to go and see dead chickens everywhere?" Simon shook his head as he stepped onto the balcony with us. "I'd rather go run in some woods and do some killing of my own than walk into a place like that."

"Of course, you would," Evan mumbled as he moved over to sit next to me. He glanced at me out of the corner of his eye and nodded.

He had the same concerns as Liam and me.

"Maybe next time you visit; we'll take you to see the plant." Mr. Buckley nodded. "But not this time."

His voice held alpha will within it as if he thought he could slip it by us. I noticed Micah tense, but Simon was behind me eating. He then propped his feet on the back of my chair, making his shoes dig into my back.

The asshole was focused more on being an ass to me than what was actually going on around him.

I turned around, grabbed his leg, and stared into his eyes, letting my wolf come forward. "Do it one more time, and Evan won't have to beat your ass. I will."

Something shifted in Simon as his eyes met mine. He huffed out a breath but put his feet back on the ground.

Between the chicken processing factory and Simon, my night was going to be full. I was really getting tired of everyone pushing me around.

CHAPTER FIFTEEN

Once again, we were dropped off at another fancy hotel in downtown Atlanta. The Four Seasons felt very similar to the one we had stayed at in New York. Once again, Liam and I got our own room while the boys shared a suite down the hall.

The bedspread was white, and the table that sat in the corner was a modern black. Directly across from the bed was light gray cabinetry that had drawers we could use, and a flat-screen television hung so that we could easily watch from the bed or the table.

"Do you ever feel guilty for staying in places like these?" I wasn't trying to shame him, but it was hard being surrounded by luxury after what I had seen in New York.

"Not really." Liam walked out of the marble bathroom with dark tile flooring and pulled me into his arms. "You have to remember; it's part of our job."

"Living in luxury is our job?" I needed to know how he was going to rationalize his thinking.

"Well, yes and no." He nodded his head toward the

window. "It's the same way humans work. The ones who get the most important and hardest jobs get paid the most."

"But we were born into it." We hadn't worked our way up the ladder, so to speak.

"Just like a lot of people who inherit money." Liam kissed the top of my forehead. "You do realize how our life will change once we ascend the council. We'll be working all the time and rarely have downtime. It's one of the most demanding jobs in the world. If done right, we will be able to help our people become stronger and wealthier, and we can't do it without our financial backing. So even if we're staying in a nice hotel room, that doesn't change who we are and what our future accomplishes. We have to have private planes to travel and attend to the packs' needs easily. We stay in more luxurious hotel rooms, mainly for the extra security. It's a privilege for all the sacrifices we have to make in the name of protecting our packs."

It kind of made sense, but it still didn't sit well with me. Maybe it was because I grew up without all the extra fluff. "So... what are our plans tonight?"

"We're going to go visit a chicken processing factory." He arched an eyebrow as his blue eyes stared right at me. "Is that what you're getting at?"

"Maybe." He knew me all too well. They should've been eager to show us even if it was only a drive-by. It was like they expected us to be impressed by the profits and move on.

"Well, let's get going. I looked it up, and Gainesville is about an hour away." Liam took out his phone, but before he could type out a message, there was a knock on our door.

I pulled out of his arms and headed to the door. When I opened it, I wasn't surprised to see the three heirs. Granted, Simon was in the back, leaning against the wall, frowning.

Liam put his phone back in his pocket. "I was about to text you. Mia and I made some plans and I was letting you guys know..."

"That you're going to the chicken processing factory." Evan cut Liam off, but there was a twinkle in his eyes. "That's what I figured. We're in."

"Technically, I'm being forced." Simon frowned and shook his head. "Why the hell do you idiots want to go to a chicken processing factory? It sounds disgusting. Even worse than that apartment building in New York."

"You don't have to go." In fact, I'd rather he stayed behind. He seemed to be getting more and more ornery the longer we were all together.

"That's exactly why I'm going." Simon narrowed his eyes at me. "You're messing with their heads. If it weren't for you, we'd be going out to dinner and relaxing."

"Stop being an ass." Liam stood beside me and took my hand in his. "If it weren't for her, we wouldn't be seeing some of the struggles our people are going through."

"All this is going to do is cause problems." Simon lifted both hands in the air. "Don't you see it? It's going to cause the regional and city alphas to get pissed off."

"So what?" He was acting like he wanted to stay in denial. "They aren't performing their jobs."

"Like you know shit about what their jobs are." Simon sneered and wrinkled his nose as if he was disgusted. "You need to go back to your stupid-ass pack and leave us the hell alone."

"Dude, you've gone too far." Micah sighed the words as Liam pushed through the group and reared back, punching Simon in the face.

"Dammit." Simon grabbed his nose as blood poured out

of it. Anger flickered in his eyes as he glared at me. "I hate you. This is what you've done to us."

"No, it's you." Evan flanked me on one side. "You're the problem."

Liam stood on my other side so that I was in the center, protected.

The thing was I didn't need their protection. Something was going to explode between Simon and me, and the more they got involved, the worse it was going to be.

"I have to agree with them." Micah's shoulders sagged as if it pained him to admit the truth. "If people aren't being treated right, we need to know."

"Why?" Simon pinched the bridge of his nose as blood poured down his shirt. "They're weak, so why should it matter? Only the strong need to survive."

There it was. The truth about how he felt. He didn't give a shit if his people were struggling, and I had a feeling that was how the current council felt too. "Because it should matter. That was the whole reason the council was created, to begin with."

"Look, just stay here." Micah patted his friend on the shoulder. "But I need to see what's going on with my people with my own eyes."

"I'm not going to get left behind." Simon headed back down to the next room. "We're supposed to be doing this together. Let me change my shirt." He went into the room and shut the door.

"I wish he'd just stay here." Liam frowned as he took my hand in his. "He's a wild card."

"He is, but we've grown up together and will lead together." Micah glanced at me. "Bringing in Mia changed the dynamics of the group. You know he hates change."

And we're questioning your parents. I squeezed Liam's hand. *So that's even more change. He's having a hard time.*

"He still doesn't need to be an ass though," Evan said as he ran a hand down his face. "He's got to grow up at some point."

The door opened again, and Simon came out with a new polo shirt on. It was blood-red with the wolf and moon in silver—the standard logo for Wolf Moon.

"At least, if I need to punch you in the nose again, the blood will blend in with your shirt." Liam's voice was filled with anger.

"Let's just go." Simon pushed through the group and headed to the elevator. "The sooner we get there, the sooner we'll get back. I don't have the energy or the time for this shit."

Well, okay then. The four of us followed behind him.

LUCKILY, we were able to determine which chicken processing plant was the one the alphas had been referring to. The owner of the plant was Mr. Haggard himself, so it was easy to find.

Micah had a Navigator rented and waiting for us outside the hotel, so we were able to leave without anyone noticing.

Simon sat in the very back while Liam and I sat in the middle row. Micah drove the car, and Evan sat up front, grunting when Micah was about to take a bad turn. Apparently, Micah wasn't very good at following directions.

We parked in the back of the factory since there were no gates, which I found odd. The building wasn't anything amazing. It was a cement building that was meant to stand the test of time. There were two doors in the back that backed up to a section of huge garbage cans. The cans were in a gated area and locked so no one could come and dump trash there.

"Damn, this stinks," Simon whined from the backseat.

I wasn't surprised it came from him.

"What did you expect?" Liam rolled his eyes. "It's a chicken processing plant, for fuck's sake."

The second I climbed out of the car, one of the back doors to the building opened, and someone rolled a large cart out to the garbage. *Now's our chance.*

The five of us walked across the parking lot and waited for the person, a woman, to turn around and go back inside.

After a few minutes, she reappeared and headed to the door that led back into the building. When her eyes landed on us, she stopped in place. "What do you want?" Her voice shivered with fear.

As I took in the young woman, I noted that she looked worse than the residents had in New York. She had a young voice, but her body sagged as if she barely had any energy. Her eyes were so sunken in that it looked as if she could easily be on drugs, but their scent wasn't in the air. Her hair was greasy and pulled away from her face. She was about my height but at least thirty pounds lighter than me.

"Mr. Haggard told us about the plant, so we wanted to drop in and check it out.'" I had no clue what to say to her, but the other four guys were tense and came off intimidating as hell. "We're here for a visit and will be heading out tomorrow."

"Who are you?" Her eyes glanced from me to the other heirs, one by one. "He didn't tell us you were coming." Her voice shook even more.

I glanced at Micah, waiting for him to shine. After all, this was his territory.

His golden eyes widened as he cleared his throat. "I'm Micah Croft, the heir to the Southern Blood Council position," he said as he pointed at each heir he introduced, "and that one is Simon Green over the west, Evan Rafferty over the east, and Liam Hale over the north."

Her eyes seemed to bulge from her head as they landed back on me. "And you are?"

For the first time in my life, I wanted to say the Overseer. Somehow, I forced other words through my lips. "I'm Mia Davis."

"My fated mate." Liam appeared next to me and held my hand. "We were hoping to see what Mr. Haggard and Mr. Buckley were going on and on about."

"Uh... Let me call him." Her face, a light olive complexion, turned pale. "I mean... I have to get permission."

"To let the heirs to The Blood Council in a plant that technically belongs to us?" Evan arched an eyebrow as he stared her down.

I hated that he was intimidating her, but he wanted the same thing as I did. To go in there without Mr. Haggard or Mr. Buckley knowing until after we were done.

"Oh, I..." She took a step back.

"Let us in now." Micah pointed to the door. "We won't stay long and promise not to interfere with your work."

Her shoulders slouched, but she nodded her head in defeat.

The problem was her wolf appeared stronger than this. When she met my eyes, she didn't divert her gaze automatically. It was as if her spirit was broken.

She hurried back to the door and entered the code on a

keypad. The door unlocked, and when I took a step inside, I stopped right in my tracks.

The room was huge, at least twenty thousand square feet. Dead chickens hung from metal connected hangers on a track suspended from the ceiling. The room had three sets of them, holding what appeared to be thousands of chickens in one place.

Blood slicked the entire floor. So much so that it was hard not to slip. Everyone was dressed in white clothing stained and soaked through with blood.

As I took in each and every person, they appeared the same as the girl. They moved lethargically, and their physiques were skin and bones.

"Who are you?" An older man approached us, the stench of dead chicken nearly covering the scent of his wolf. "Why did you let these people in here, Amelia?"

"Dad, I didn't know what else to do." She took in a deep breath as her head snapped in our direction. "They are the heirs to The Blood Council."

"Oh..." He lifted both hands in the air, and fear showed on his face. "We've been working to catch up for the last twenty hours. There is only so much we can do though."

"What are you talking about?" Micah's forehead wrinkled.

"The line went down last night, and we got behind. We're catching up." He waved his hands, signifying that the people should continue working. There were several people adding chickens to the hangers. "We've been working nonstop like usual."

"That's not why we're here." Micah took a deep breath and winced at the foul air he sucked in. It smelled a lot like what I thought rotting corpses would. "We wanted to check on all of you."

"Don't say things you don't mean." The man laughed, but it soon turned into a cough. "We will catch up. No need to take it out on our families."

"What do you mean?" Something bigger was at play here, and we needed to find out what it was.

"You're trying to tell me you don't know that the reason every one of us is in here is all because we voiced a concern about our alpha's decision?" He surveyed the group as if he was searching for something.

"No, we do not." Micah's voice was deeper than normal.

"What do you expect if you're rising up against your leaders?" Simon scoffed and shook his head.

"We didn't. We only voiced our concerns about certain decisions." The old man huffed. "They wanted to increase our taxes. My daughter and I voiced that we couldn't afford it. Now, we're here paying off the debt. That's what happened to everyone here. You can't disagree, or you'll receive punishment while they hold the lives of your family over your heads."

I can't believe this. Liam shook his head and turned his eyes back to the factory floor.

The five of us began walking around, our shoes sloshing in the pools of liquid on the ground. This was one time I was happy that I wore tennis shoes, but I didn't think they'd be salvageable after all of this.

As we walked by each person, they busily worked, doing their best not to meet our eyes. It was as if they were trying to pretend we didn't exist. When we got to one of the doors, the man from earlier appeared in front of it.

"There, are you satisfied?" He stood there and crossed his arms.

He was acting as if he was blocking the door from us. "No, we'd like to see in there."

"There's nothing in there." He shook his head and pointed at the door. "Thanks for your visit, but we have a lot left to do."

Liam nodded at me and walked around the man, throwing the door open. He stopped in his tracks, and his shoulders slouched at what he saw through the door.

I hurried around and rubbed my eyes, sure that what I was seeing had to be a mistake. It was another large room about half the size of the one behind us where the dead chickens hung. However, this one held hundreds of hammocks hanging from the ceiling. There were at least two hundred people sleeping in them, all still wearing the white clothes they wore to work in with blood-soaked through.

"Are they off duty?" I had a feeling the answer was going to break my heart.

"Yes, as if you don't know." There was no anger in his words. "We work sixteen-hour days and sleep here. They leave food in the kitchen, but not enough for all the workers, so we have to split and make sure people get equal portions."

"Why don't the stronger wolves take the food and let the others starve?" Simon's brows furrowed, not understanding the humanity these wolves showed by making sure each person was treated equally. Something that every member of The Blood Council should know and understand.

"Because we are one pack and take care of all." The old man shook his head and sighed. "Something that you elites have forgotten all about."

"What about clean clothes?" They had to at least change clothes every now and then.

"Once a week, we sacrifice a little sleep to get clean and change. Most of the time, we're too tired to do anything after a long shift." His eyes landed on me, and I might have caught a small glimmer of hope within their depths. "Are you going to be a part of the council? I thought it was only those four?" he asked as he pointed to the heirs.

"Like hell she is," Simon laughed. "She's only a mate ... to Liam."

"But that is good too." His eyes landed on my mate.

"We've got to go." Evan nodded back toward the door.

"But..." I didn't want to leave them. I wanted to do something for them like we were able to in New York.

The best thing we can do is leave and hope that Haggard and Buckley don't find out. Liam took my hand and pulled me toward the door. *We have to get home and make changes for them. They can't leave here, and if they do, it'll cause a civil war.*

Good, maybe a civil war is needed. The rebellion group had formed, and now we all knew why.

But why have a civil war when we can change things? Liam glanced around. *Look?*

My eyes tore from the hammocks and back into the room where all the others worked. Fear shone clear in their eyes as they kept trying to focus on their goal.

"I think it's best if you go. You're distracting us, which will only make us have to work longer and harder. We have nowhere else to go, and we couldn't find any other work. That's how we ended up here." The old man's shoulders slumped, and he gave me a sad smile. "But please, don't forget what you all saw. We need help."

My eyes teared up as Liam gently pulled me away, and the five of us headed back out the door to our freedom. A freedom that none of these people had. The old man slowly followed us to the door, and right before Evan closed it, I searched the older man out again. "I promise," I vowed as the door shut, cutting me off from them.

CHAPTER SIXTEEN

W hen I woke up the next morning, the stench of the chicken processing plant was still stuck in my nose. I'd showered over and over last night, trying to erase the smell, but it didn't happen. It probably had more to do with my memories than anything else.

"Are you already awake?" Liam pulled my back closer to his chest. "You didn't sleep well last night. Why don't you go back to sleep?"

Well, you're up too. I didn't have the energy to actually talk, using our mind link instead. I glanced over at the clock and saw that it was six in the morning. *Besides, the alarm is going to go off in thirty minutes.*

There was a loud knock on the door, and Micah's voice called, "Are you two up?"

See, no point in going back to sleep. I hated to crawl out of his arms, but Micah sounded a little upset. I walked over to my bag and picked it up, taking it into the bathroom. *I'll be out in a second if you don't mind answering him.*

Yeah, okay. Liam crawled out of bed, looking sexy as

hell. He grabbed a shirt from the table next to him and put it on, covering his bare chest. "Give me a second."

I hated that we didn't have a little one-on-one time, but after what we saw last night, we were out of sorts. Even Simon was quiet, which was a change. Granted, I wasn't sure if it was because of his displeasure with me or what he actually saw. Knowing him, I was leaning toward the first option.

When I closed the door, I slipped out of my pajamas and into a pair of jeans and a sweater. We were heading to Chicago today, and it was cooler than the south. I quickly brushed my hair and teeth and put on some light makeup before heading back out to the main room.

Micah was sitting on the couch and frowning. He glanced at me and gave me a sad smile. "I'm sorry for bothering you guys, but I was hoping we could go downstairs and eat together. I couldn't sleep last night, but I didn't want to hear Simon's commentary if I tried talking to him and Evan."

"No problem." My stomach growled in response to his words. We hadn't stopped for dinner after what we saw, and no one mentioned eating. All of us had to be on the same page.

"Let me run to the bathroom and change." Liam headed to the bathroom, picking up his bag on the way by.

"Are you okay?" It was clear what his answer was, but I wanted to see if he'd admit it.

His face was lined with worry, and his shoulders were slumped. There were dark circles under his eyes, which told me he didn't sleep well last night. Mine had been similar, but I was able to use makeup to cover it up.

"No, I'm not." He sighed, somehow slumping even more. "I'm having a hard time believing my dad doesn't know about it, but at the same time, he couldn't be letting that happen," he said as his eyes caught mine, "could he?"

I wanted to scream of course he knows, but Micah seemed shell shocked. It didn't feel right to pull the rug out from under him. Our relationship was still a little shaky, so I didn't want to ruin what little ground we had in common. "I can't answer that."

Liam stepped out of the bathroom dressed and looking fine as hell. He wore navy blue slacks and a light blue button-down shirt. It made his eyes stand out even more than usual.

However, I was jealous. It took him less than five minutes to get ready whereas it took me at least twenty.

"Are Evan and Simon meeting us down there?" Liam headed over to us.

"Yeah, I needed a second away. Simon had already started up this morning." Micah stood, dressed much like his mood. He wore a pair of black slacks and a black polo shirt. "I needed a break."

Didn't we all? I forced a small smile across my face. "Let's go eat. Maybe he is hangry."

"Maybe." Micah shrugged and opened the door.

Breakfast had been strangely quiet for the five of us, and soon we were back on the plane. We'd all been focused on eating what was on our plates instead of discussing anything. The one time Micah had brought up last night, Simon started getting loud, so Liam shut it down. We were around humans, and we didn't need to risk them over-hearing.

We took our usual spots on the plane and were soon up in the sky.

Micah kept his eye on Simon, and when he was immersed in his show, he took a deep breath and said, "Do you think we're going to be able to help those people?"

"I'm assuming you mean all of those we've discovered so far on this trip?" Liam arched an eyebrow.

"Yeah, I mean the council can't know, right?" Micah shook his head as if he was trying to make it true. "They couldn't."

"Our dads are alpha asshole jerks." Evan narrowed his eyes at Micah. "Are you so sure about that?"

"Well, we are assholes too, and we didn't know." Micah's voice filled with hope.

He didn't want to believe everything he saw, but you can't deny the facts when they are staring you straight in your face.

I hoped those two cities were the exceptions. They were large and able to hide things better, but my gut said otherwise. "Why don't we go see the last two cities, and we can always go from there." I hoped I was wrong and that everything was normal.

"Yeah, I guess that's a fair request." Micah's shoulders seemed to relax some like he was looking for anything positive to put his mind at ease. "They could be the outlier."

The rest of the plane ride passed in complete silence.

CHICAGO WAS one of the main cities of the North, which included North Dakota, South Dakota, Nebraska, and Kansas on to the right until it touched the borders of the south and north. This was the territory that Liam represented.

When we got off the plane there and stepped into the private side of the airport, I wasn't surprised to find two towering male alphas again. Out of every city we went to, I had yet to find a female one, which didn't sit well with me. I understood that males were generally stronger, but female leaders were just as tough, albeit in different ways.

Liam wrapped an arm around my waist as we approached the two towering males. This was Liam's area, and even though he hadn't told me in words, his actions showed he was ensuring that everyone knew we were a team and a package deal.

"Mr. Hale." Kai's father stood right in front of us. He was the more muscular of the two and was in his mid-forties. He had Kai's facial structure; only his eyes were light blue instead of brown, and he had reddish hair. "Ms. Davis, what a surprise." His eyebrows raised as he looked at me.

"I'm sure my father told you she was with me." Liam stiffened as he stared him down.

"Actually, no, he didn't." Mr. Thorn kept his eyes on me. "But it seems you both have claimed one another. I'm assuming Kai knows."

"Yes, he does." I didn't want his father to think I was leading Kai on or something.

The thinner one held his hands out to Liam and cleared his throat. "Hello, Mr. Hale." His gray suit bunched around his shoulders as he and Liam shook hands. "It's great to see you and the other heirs again." His charcoal eyes met mine. "And to meet your mate." He didn't bother extending his hand out to me. "Your father did, in fact, inform me that she was in tow." A snide smile crossed his face as he stared Mr. Thorn down.

"Why am I not surprised? Mr. Keith." Liam arched an eyebrow at him.

Shouldn't Kai's dad know before him? This whole interaction was strange, and I couldn't quite put a finger on why.

Mr. Thorn and my dad's relationship is tense, to say the least. Mr. Keith here is vying for the regional position. But he can't flat-out challenge Mr. Thorn because of how things work. Liam's expression stayed neutral even though the bond told me he was aggravated. *That's partially why Kai and I have tension. Dad is strategically determining how to have Mr. Thorn step down without forcing it and causing chaos. If people think we aren't making sure things stay in a certain order, more people would be vying for a higher alpha position, which could cause civil unrest.*

"Well, you know me and your father talk daily." The city alpha arched his eyebrow at Mr. Thorn. "How often do you talk with him?"

"I talk to him quite frequently too." Mr. Thorn cleared his throat and glanced at me once more. "I hate to run, but there were things that came up today, so I won't be able to stay with you right now. But next time you visit Chicago, I'll make sure that I can personally show you around."

"Is everything okay?" Liam's brows furrowed. *That's really strange.*

"It's fine. Something just came up." Mr. Thorn turned to Mr. Keith. "I'm assuming you can take it from here?"

"Of course." He chuckled in response. "I'll gladly keep them company. I thought it might be best for them to come by my house so we could talk about business undisturbed."

"Very well. I'm going to take off." Mr. Thorn's eyes kept focusing back on me. "Call me if you need anything, but I really need to go attend to something personal." He shook the other three heirs' hands and headed straight to the door.

"Is Kai all right?" My words made his father pause.

As he turned to me, something passed through his eyes. "Yes, he's fine. Thanks for asking, it's something else." He turned on his heel, heading out the door.

"Well, that's quite surprising. Who would've thought something would be more important than meeting with our future leaders?" The city alpha tsked and shook his head. "It's a good thing I had everything planned anyway. Let's go. There is a limo waiting for us."

Is it normal for Mr. Thorn to take off like that? Every alpha had taken this so seriously. Something important must be going on.

No, it's not. Liam glanced over his shoulders at the other heirs. "Let's go."

Within minutes, we were in the car and pulling away from the airport.

AFTER A SEVERAL HOUR tour around the city, we pulled into an extensive, gated subdivision that backed up to some woods. There was a huge clubhouse in the center with a pool attached. As we drove through, it was clear each house had to be worth at least a million dollars. Soon, we passed every house, closing in on the largest brick one on the end.

We pulled into the driveway, and the limo driver jumped out and hurried to let us out of the car. As we climbed out, the tall wooden front door opened, revealing a gorgeous woman who was close to Mr. Keith's age. She had long, cascading red hair, and her skin held a light olive complexion. Not quite as light as Simon's but still on the lighter end of the spectrum. Her huge green eyes were gorgeous and could be seen even from where we stood. She had on a long, hunter green dress, and her lips were painted close to the same shade as her hair.

"And this," Mr. Keith said as he headed to the front steps that led inside, "is my gorgeous wife and mate."

The five of us followed behind him.

She lowered her head ever so slightly to each one of us, and when her eyes met mine, she smiled. "It's nice to see another woman in the mix."

"There are always women in the mix, Gretchen." Mr. Keith's tone was slightly cold and disapproving. His eyes landed on the rest of the group. "We value women here."

"They just aren't men." Simon lifted his nose in the air as he side-eyed me.

"Exactly." The alpha chuckled as he entered the house.

"Stop being an asshole," Liam growled at Simon as the loose cannon pushed through our group.

He'd been frowning and unengaged the entire time until now. More and more frequently, he took any opportunity to insult or attempt to hurt me.

"Leave him alone." Evan shook his head. "It's only encouraging him."

That was probably true. Liam and I followed Micah into the house.

If I'd thought I'd seen grand things before, they didn't compare to this place, which blew my mind. The whole entrance was marble with a set of curved stairways on each side of the room.

"I'll get the driver to bring in your things." Mr. Keith pointed upstairs. "We have plenty of room for all of you to stay here tonight if you'd like, instead of a hotel room. Each person could have their own room and bathroom upstairs."

"That sounds great." Liam grinned.

"Perfect." Mr. Keith turned back around as an older shifter gentleman walked out in what could only be called butler gear. "Please go get their things and place them in the rooms upstairs. Also, please ensure *the girl's* stuff is put in the same room with Mr. Hale."

'The girl' was said condescendingly. I wanted to say something, but I bit my tongue.

"Of course, Sir." The butler bowed his head. "And lunch is ready if you'd like to eat."

We followed him down a long hallway, and he turned to enter a huge dining room. The table was black and modern with seating for at least twenty. The plates were already placed so that four sat on one side and three on the other.

Liam took my hand and sat on the side that had four. He sat on one end and placed me in between him and Evan again. As we sat down, Micah joined our side while Simon, the alpha, and his mate sat across from us.

It wasn't long before they served our food, which was a medium-rare steak and potatoes.

As we all dug in, Gretchen cut a piece of steak off. Before she could put it in her mouth, it fell off her fork and into her lap. She gasped and shook her head. "I'm so sorry."

"Clean it up." Mr. Keith growled, causing unease to rise around the table.

"It was an accident." She took her napkin and cleaned off her dress as best she could.

"It's okay." This whole situation was being blown way out of proportion. I wanted to point out she had only dropped something, but I had a feeling it would only irritate the city alpha further.

"No, it's not." Mr. Keith's sharp tone was directed at me

as he narrowed his eyes on me. "A woman should have grace and poise at all times."

"They're also human, part animal, and make mistakes." Liam stiffened in his chair. "Just like men do."

"Not on my watch." Mr. Keith growled as he stared at his mate with something akin to disgust in his eyes.

Gretchen flinched, and her lips quivered as she tried to smooth her expressions into one of indifference.

Just let it go. I didn't want to get into a huge fight with the city alpha here. Mr. Hale was already pissed at Liam; I didn't want to make things worse.

He can't speak to you like that. "You may not address my mate in that tone again. Do you understand?" Liam's jaw was clenched.

"Of course, Sir." The alpha's voice was short, and he averted his eyes.

"He's a little touchy about her." Simon glanced over at the city alpha.

"Simon." Micah's eyes widened, and he shook his head.

"What?" Simon shrugged his shoulders. "It's true. He's..."

"Shut the fuck up." Evan's voice was low and heated. "Or I'll make you."

"Look what you've done." Mr. Keith shook his head. "Why don't you and Mr. Hale's mate go do something while we finish talking here?"

You don't have to go. Liam reached over and took my hand in his. *You haven't eaten since breakfast either.*

"Of course, dear." Her voice trembled with her submission.

No, I think I should. Something isn't right here. This house looked too perfect along with everything in it. For him to blow up at her for a little mistake appeared asinine. *I don't want him to direct more anger her way.* I rose and turned, following Gretchen down the long hallway.

"I'm so sorry about that. You know how they are." She laughed without humor, and soon we entered a huge living room with white furniture and dark cherry wood floors. She walked over and sat on the end of the couch.

"I'm not sure what you mean by how they are." I moved so I sat on the other side of the couch and looked at her.

"Oh, shit. You don't know what you're getting into, do you?" Her green eyes turned somber. "You'll learn soon enough when the newness of the mate bond wears off."

"What do you mean?" Her words filled me with trepidation.

Her green eyes seemed haunted. "Things aren't always what they seem."

Something shifted inside of me. This was an abused woman speaking to me. I would know; my dad took one in who had been on the run. I didn't have proof, but I would by the end of the night.

CHAPTER SEVENTEEN

"Mr. Hale, you haven't even finished lunch." Mr. Keith's voice called from the hall.

"If my mate doesn't eat, neither do I," Liam said as he turned the corner, entering the room Gretchen and I were in.

It's fine. Go eat. I had a feeling that by making a bigger deal of it, it was going to be worse on Gretchen.

No, if you go without, so do I. He walked over to where I sat and stood next to me.

It wasn't long before the other four joined us in the room.

Mr. Keith's face turned a slight red hue as his hateful eyes landed on his wife. "That's fine. We can make up for it at dinner. I have the pack coordinating a dinner so you can meet everyone."

"That sounds like a plan," Liam said as he turned his back toward me, keeping me out of Mr. Keith's view.

"Well then, why don't you all go upstairs and make yourselves at home. Maybe relax a little." Mr. Keith smiled, but it didn't reflect in his eyes. "This will give me time to take care of a few things and get ready for dinner. We can go down in an hour or so. That way, you'll have enough time to meet every member of my pack. I'm sure you'll be more than impressed by them, unlike my mate."

"You do realize no one..." Liam started.

"Thank you, that sounds good." Evan cut Liam off and nodded at Micah.

"We've been traveling with little downtime, so that would be nice." Micah grimaced as he glanced at each one of us.

The tension in the room was practically suffocating.

No one wanted to make the first move, so I took my mate's hand. "Let's go rest so they can plan. A quick nap might do us some good."

"Also, we have a greenhouse garden in the back that is quite exquisite if you'd like to venture out at some point." Mr. Keith's smile spread wide. "We like to grow herbs and such to have only the freshest ingredients on hand. It's quite something to take in."

"We will definitely take you up on that." We needed to stroke his ego right now because there was something akin to a maddening gleam in his eyes.

"Come on." Liam tugged me gently with his hand. "Let's go get settled in first."

The heirs followed behind us, and Simon grumbled loud enough so we could hear, "I still would've liked to eat, dammit. Another damn thing she's ruined."

Liam's body stiffened, and anger flared through our bond.

He's trying to rile you up. I squeezed his hand, attempting to calm him down. *He's feeling alienated from the three of you, and he's acting out, trying to cause more trouble between you and your father. Don't fall for it.*

Still, it pisses me off. Liam took a deep breath and turned the corner so we were climbing the stairs to the second level. *He's always been a pain in the ass, but not this bad.*

When we reached the top of the stairway, we walked down a white hallway with dark cherry wood floors. There were two rooms to the left and two on the right.

A butler came out from the far right room, and his eyes widened when he found us. "Oh, I didn't realize you'd be done so soon."

"We can set up our own rooms. It's no bother." The last thing I wanted to do was get another person on Mr. Keith's bad side.

"Oh, it's all done." He chuckled. "You only startled me. My old ears don't hear quite as well as they used to. I used to think it was a curse, but I'm learning it's a blessing." His eyes turned cloudy. "Anyway, this room," he said as he pointed at the one he had just exited, "is yours and Mr. Hale's." He then pointed at the door right next to ours. "Mr. Rafferty, I put your luggage in there while Mr. Green's is the door across the hall from Mr. Hale's, and Mr. Croft's is right across from Mr. Rafferty. However, if any of you want to switch, that is between you four." The butler nodded his head and hurried toward the stairs, disappearing.

"Let's take ten minutes to get settled, and then we'll go look around." Liam motioned for me to go into our room first.

As I stepped into the bedroom, my breath caught. It was much larger than I imagined. In the center of the spacious area was a huge canopy bed made of dark wood. A crystal chandelier hung down from the center of the ceiling. The rest of the furniture was made of matching wood but cut in a sleek, modern style.

"Holy crap. I've never seen anything this nice." I spun around, taking in the entire thing.

Liam chuckled, and adoration filled our bond. "You're like a breath of fresh air sometimes." He walked over and wrapped his arms around my waist. "If you like it so much, we can buy something similar back home."

"But we live in the dorms." Him talking about our future home made my heart speed up.

"I'm talking about when we take over the council." A tender smile spread across his face. "We won't be living in the dorms indefinitely."

It was probably a bad thing that I hadn't really thought about my next steps after school. Obviously, it was the council, but I hadn't thought much past that. "It's nice— don't get me wrong, but isn't it kind of... obnoxious?"

"Like wealth being shoved in your face?" Liam arched an eyebrow.

"Exactly." I understood his point about living in luxury, but at some point, it was downright obnoxious. All that money could go back and benefit all the packs. It seemed a bit over-the-top. "All I know is when someone tries so hard to have perfect things, they are hiding something."

"Yeah, I'd agree with that." Liam snorted. "I mean, look at how our dads raised us. We're all fucked up in our own way, but we have to appear as the perfect heirs."

"You aren't fucked up." I never would've imagined he thought that of himself. He may have made mistakes, but hell, we'd all done that.

"Not since I made the best decision in my life." He brushed his fingertips across my cheek.

I stood on my tiptoes and pressed my lips to his. *You did it all on your own. I was only here for support and to call you out when you acted stupid.*

Tell me how you really feel? He chuckled against my lips.

I hated to ruin the moment, but I thought we needed to go look around. I had a feeling if we looked in the right places, we might find some answers. It seemed as if the whole purpose of the tour was going to blow up in the council's face. Evan was proving himself to be more loyal to me than I expected, and poor Micah's eyes were beginning to open. Simon was the only one who still didn't seem to give a shit, which was a whole other issue we'd have to address at another time.

Let's go. Liam's shoulders sagged. *Is it sad that I hoped my region would be different?*

Nope. I pulled away from his lips and stared into his beautiful blue eyes. *That just means you care.*

THE HEIRS HAD MET up with us, and we toured the greenhouse as Mr. Keith suggested. It did contain herbs but also other beautiful flowers that could only survive in the summer heat. As I walked along the edge of the backyard, away from all the greenery, something caught my ear.

"You better make sure tonight goes well after your fuck up at lunch." Mr. Keith's words were full of disgust and rage.

Liam, come here. I wanted him to see it for himself. The last thing I needed was for Simon to call me a liar and force the group to pull further apart. I walked over to the edge of the window and peered inside. It had to be his study. There was a large bookcase to the side and a huge, dark wooden desk in the middle of the room where Mr. Keith could stare at the doorway with two chairs in front of the desk.

Gretchen sat in one of the seats and was now dressed in a black dress with silver heels. Mr. Keith wore the same thing from earlier, but his face wasn't holding anything back.

I'll follow your scent. Liam's voice appeared in my head.

Within seconds, I heard four sets of footsteps approaching behind me.

"I didn't mean to drop the piece of steak." Gretchen's voice was full of angst. "It was an accident."

"We don't have accidents here. You know that." Mr. Keith leaned over his desk with rage clear on his face. He towered over his trembling mate with pure hate in his eyes. "Your only job is to be perfect. Why the fuck is that so hard for you?"

A door opened, and a tall man similar to Mr. Keith appeared, but he was several years younger. His dark hair was close to the same shade as his eyes. "You called, my alpha?"

"I'm sorry to burden you with women problems." Mr. Keith shook his head. "But as my right-hand man, I need you to oversee that this dinner goes perfectly. Make sure each lady is in line because my own fucking mate can't keep her shit together."

"Speaking of which, did you know that she and my mate got drunk the other night?" The dark man wrinkled his nose. "They stumbled on their way home from the club-house, and Beth messed up a pair of her dress pants."

So Mr. Keith wasn't the only one who viewed things this way; his beta did too, which meant probably every single man in his pack treated their mates or even young daughters like this.

"You did what?" Mr. Keith's voice was so loud it hurt my ears even from where I stood. "You went out in public like that?"

"It was just our pack ..." But even as she said the words, her body shrank down into the chair. "We hadn't eaten that day, and it took us by surprise."

"That's no excuse. When the heirs leave tomorrow morning, there will be hell to pay." He pulled at his jacket and glanced at his beta once more. "Please, help me take care of this. I need to go search for the heirs and keep them preoccupied until it's time for dinner. Make sure no one messes up."

"Of course." The dark man bowed his head and sneered at Gretchen. "Come on, bitch. We have things to do."

Let's go. He's heading this way. Liam took my hand and tugged me away.

"What's the big deal?" Simon scoffed as he hurried back to the greenhouse. "He just wants to make a good impression. That's how everyone should be."

"They should treat their mates like garbage?" Evan crossed his arms as he stared Simon down.

"That's not right, man." Micah shook his head.

"Hell, we treat people that way." Simon lifted both hands in the air. "In fact, we even treated her that way," he said as he pointed to me.

"We only treat people that way when they haven't proven themselves to us." Liam's eyes darkened. "Everyone wants to use us for something, so that's why we treat them that way. I was a dumbass who tried fighting our bond, and I did things I regret to this day."

"Mr. Hale." Mr. Keith appeared from the house and smiled at us. "Will all of you be ready to go soon? My people are putting their finishing touches on everything now."

Liam turned toward him. "Sure, I can't wait to meet the others."

WE'D BEEN at the gathering for over an hour, and nothing much had happened. It was all pleasantries and talking about the weather.

"So, how long have you and Mr. Hale been bonded?" Gretchen asked as a woman with light blonde hair and blue eyes appeared next to me.

"Not quite two months." Even though it had only been a short amount of time, it felt like we'd known each other longer. We'd been through so much together.

"Well, he is a catch." The woman held out her hand and smiled. "I'm Beth. The mate to Mr. Keith's beta, Tommy."

So, this is the woman Gretchen had gotten drunk with the other night. "Nice to meet you. I'm Mia."

"Are you having a good time?" Gretchen glanced around the place at all the people who were mingling together.

A familiar hand touched my lower back. "Thought you might like a glass of wine." Liam grinned as he handed it to me.

"Thank you." I smiled at him and took a small sip.

"That wine is the finest that you can get." Mr. Keith appeared next to Liam and nodded. "We only serve the best here."

"It's quite delicious." It was, but it hurt to admit it. I glanced around, noting that I was the only woman in jeans. All of the women either wore designer dresses or dress pants that were of the latest fashion. Even the young girls were dressed immaculately, and I noticed not one of them ate any of the food. They were quiet and had only spoken when they absolutely must. There was a dull lifelessness in their eyes.

"There are a lot of calories in that glass. Maybe you shouldn't drink the whole thing." Mr. Keith arched an eyebrow at me.

"She can drink the whole damn thing if she wants to," Liam growled at the city alpha.

"I'm surprised that you allow her to wear jeans." Tommy appeared beside Mr. Keith and shook his head in disapproval.

"Oh, they've only been mated for two months," Beth said as if that explained everything.

"It doesn't matter if it'd been fifty years; my mate can drink, eat, or wear whatever the hell she wants to." Liam's jaw clenched, and his fingers dug slightly into my side. "If you say one more word about it, we'll be leaving here immediately. Do I make myself clear?"

Simon rolled his eyes as he watched the whole thing from the sidelines.

"Well, your fathers..." Mr. Keith's shoulders stiffened.

"We don't give a damn what our fathers say or think." Evan flanked me on the other side. "When it's our turn, we'll do things our way." His huge body was coiled, ready for a fight.

"You're both standing up for this girl?" Mr. Keith's brows furrowed. "But she's an extension of you. Don't you care about how she reflects on you?"

"She's her own person." Liam shook his head. "And I'm damn proud of that. I wouldn't have it any other way." His eyes locked on mine, and there was so much damn love in them.

"Well, that's not how we work here." Mr. Keith shook his head. "You'll see how things should be when you take over the council. There is a certain order to things. That's exactly what Mr. Thorn has been learning here recently."

What the hell did that mean? I had a feeling it wasn't good.

"Maybe he had it right all along. Either way, you should remember your place." Liam said as his eyes took on the alpha glow, making Mr. Keith avert his eyes.

The room was silent as the city alpha submitted to him.

"I think it's time for us to leave." Liam took my hand and led me to the door.

"I agree with that." Micah frowned as if it pained him to agree.

"Of course you would." Simon spat the words.

Liam didn't pause, but I glanced over my shoulder, watching the expressions on all the women's faces. Beth appeared hopeful, but Gretchen looked petrified. And that somehow broke my heart even more.

CHAPTER EIGHTEEN

As we headed out the door of the hotel we wound up staying in, we found Mr. Thorn waiting outside. His face was lined with worry, and his eyes appeared weary.

"I'm sorry that I was unavailable yesterday, so I figured it was best if I personally took you back to the airport," he said as the driver opened the back door of the limo.

"It didn't help that I pretty much demanded it." Liam carried both of our bags to the driver and set them down at his feet.

"Well, there is that." Mr. Thorn gave a tight smile. "I must say I was shocked that you didn't stay at Mr. Keith's house."

"Well, there is a damn good reason for it." Liam arched an eyebrow as if daring him to challenge him. "Mr. Keith isn't exactly the man I remembered. Staying with him was quite an eye-opener."

"Oh, Mr. Thorn, I didn't expect to see you here." Mr. Keith frowned as he took in the five of us with the regional alpha. "I'd hoped to take you to the airport and talk after what happened last night."

"We're not interested." Liam narrowed his eyes at the man. "I've asked Mr. Thorn to accompany us."

Mr. Keith's face dropped at Liam's response.

"But thank you for giving us a tour yesterday." I didn't want Liam to completely burn a bridge. He was still an alpha, at least until we could do something about it.

Don't be nice to him. Liam growled as he crawled into the limo. "Unlike my mate, I don't share those sentiments."

Soon, the others and I followed suit and climbed into the car. As always, both Evan and Liam sat on either side of me while Mr. Thorn sat between Micah and Simon.

"Is everything okay?" Liam took my hand and glanced at the regional alpha.

"It is." Mr. Thorn sighed as he glanced out the window. "I think it should be me asking you that question, though. I'm a little surprised that you don't approve of Mr. Keith. Your father sure does."

"I'm not my father." Liam's voice was low and raspy.

"Well, I'm kind of surprised because the last time I saw you, it sure seemed like you were on the same page as him." Mr. Thorn's eyes landed on me before flickering to the other three heirs. "As I'm sure the others still would agree with."

"Not all of us," Evan growled beside me.

Mr. Thorn's eyes widened. "And the other two?"

"If those bitches like being treated that way, I don't see the problem." Simon shrugged and glanced out the window as he crossed his arms.

"You're being too much." Micah leaned over Mr. Thorn, directing his words at his friend. "You've gotta stop, man."

"You guys are turning into pussies." Simon shook his head as he wrinkled his nose.

"One more word and I'll throw you out of the damn car." Liam leaned forward, ready to carry out this threat.

"You wouldn't do it." Simon snickered.

"Hell yeah, he would." Evan narrowed his eyes on Simon. "And I'll help him."

"Can't we just get along?" Micah shook his head.

"Well, if you guys weren't getting weak, there wouldn't be an issue." Simon spat the words like they tasted bitter.

Mr. Thorn sat there, watching it all with an amused expression.

"Whether the four of you like it or not, we have another stop." That was the one common goal they all still had; to inherit The Blood Council seats. "And you can't go in there acting like this." I waved my finger around to the four of them. "It's bad enough that you're doing it now."

The four of them remained silent.

"Did you get your issue resolved yesterday?" I needed to divert attention from the four heirs' relationship and back to the matters at hand.

"Yes, I was able to handle it." The corner of Mr. Thorn's lips tipped upward.

"What was the issue? Does my father know about it?" Liam took a deep breath and focused back on the regional alpha. *Thank you for getting us back on track.*

We're a team. I scooted in closer to him. *I'll always do what I can by your side.*

I love you. His words were simple but held so much meaning.

"There was a rebellion group gathering that I had to take care of." Mr. Thorn shrugged. "I figured it was better for you to hear about overall pack life in Chicago and not deal with a small rebellion that probably won't amount to anything."

Considering how things are going, it might gain momentum unless we can alter our fathers' vision. Liam took in a deep breath and breathed out. "I would've actually liked to have gone. Mr. Keith was a waste of breath."

Mr. Thorn burst out laughing. "That is something we both can agree on." His face smoothed out, and his shoulders weren't quite as tense. "Well, maybe if you're in town next time one of them happens, you can join me."

"If you were an effective alpha, there wouldn't be another meeting," Simon mumbled as he stared out the window.

"You have much to learn, Mr. Green, but you'll soon understand when you take your place on the council." Mr. Thorn frowned as he shook his head. "There will always be people trying to undermine you, no matter how much you're feared."

The cabin descended into silence for the rest of the ride to the airport.

When we climbed out of the limo at the airport, Mr. Thorn gently touched my arm.

I turned to face him as the other heirs headed to the door. I linked with Liam. *Give me a second.*

I'll stand by the door. Liam waited for me only a few yards away.

"I underestimated you." Mr. Thorn gave me a sad smile. "You're exactly what and where you need to be."

"What are you talking about?" The hairs on the back of my neck stood on end. This was the man who made me question my necklace, which led me to learn that I was the Overseer. He hadn't been thrilled with Kai's interest in me until he saw the pendant when I wore it to class, and he'd recognized the design. He approved of our relationship then, but I had completed the bond with Liam that same weekend. *He knows who I am.*

"I wasn't quite sure, but after what I've just seen, it fits even though I don't know how it's possible." His eyes seemed to lighten.

What? Liam headed over to me and glared at the alpha. "You don't know what you're talking about." Liam's voice was deep and somewhat threatening.

"Your secret is safe with me." Mr. Thorn bowed his head ever so slightly at me. "On that, you have my word. Please, if you are ever back in town, let me know. I'd love the opportunity to show you things."

"Thank you." I wasn't quite sure what else to say. We had just learned that someone knows my secret, which meant there was little time before more people learned it as well.

As WE STEPPED off the plane in Los Angeles, Simon had an extra bounce in his step. When we walked out of the huge, vibrant airport, once again we found two towering male alphas. They both had a sun-kissed complexion and appeared to be more lean and athletic than muscular.

The older one had a car salesman vibe as he nodded his head at us. He had slicked-back, brown hair and wore a strong floral cologne smell that had me close to gagging.

"Mr. Rhodes." Simon shook his hand and grinned. "So good to see you again."

"And I feel the same way, Mr. Green." He shook his hand eagerly. "And this is our city alpha, Mr. Voss." He nodded at the man right beside him.

The other man, who had red hair and green eyes, appeared to be in his late twenties. There seemed to be a hunger in them that made me uncomfortable. He scanned me from top to bottom. "It's nice to meet you, Mr. Green, and it appears you brought me a delectable present, I see."

A low growl emanated from Liam's chest. "She is my mate, so back the fuck off."

"Whoa, whoa!" He lifted both hands in the air. "I'm so sorry, but she is definitely something to marvel at. You're one lucky alpha. I'd always thought I'd never tie myself down, but I recently found someone worth doing that for."

"If you keep looking at her that way, then that will be the last thing you see." Liam stepped in front of me, blocking me from his leering eyes.

"He's awfully protective of her." Simon rolled his eyes. "I'm sorry about that."

"No problem at all." Mr. Voss held his hand out to Liam. "And you are Mr. Hale, yes?"

"Yes." Liam's answer was so rough it was almost indistinguishable, but he didn't move to shake the alpha's hand.

Mr. Voss took a step back but tried to recover by turning to Evan. "Mr. Rafferty, right?"

"Yes." Only then, a second heir refused to shake his hand.

"Wow, we must have gotten off on the wrong foot." Mr. Voss held his hand out to Micah. "How about you, Mr. Croft?"

"Yeah, hi." Micah shook the alpha's hand even though he seemed hesitant.

"All right, well, let's go. Mr. Rhodes and I thought we should take you to my home on the ocean. We have a neighborhood there that my pack lives in, and we live the life of luxury." He pointed to the limo right behind them.

We all climbed in, and within the next thirty minutes, we were pulling up to a gated community. When we passed through the gate, we drove by a few nice houses until we parked in the driveway of a house built high on a cliff that overlooked the ocean with woods directly behind the subdivision so they could shift and run.

As soon as we stepped out, the warm sun and saltwater assaulted my senses. I'd never been on the west coast before, but the water was as gorgeous as every picture I'd seen.

The house was mainly windows, and Mr. Voss headed straight to the door. "I thought you might enjoy overlooking the ocean as we talked."

"That's fine." Simon nodded at him with a huge smirk.

He was thoroughly enjoying us being on his turf right now. "Please come; we'll eat lunch and talk before we take you to your hotel for the night."

The door opened before he got to it, and when we stepped into the house, I noticed it was sleek and pristine. The girl cleaning it couldn't have been more than sixteen. When we entered the room, she turned around, and I saw fear in her eyes.

"Ah, Dee, you're doing such a good job." Mr. Voss's eyes were devoid of any emotion. "Every day you get better. Where is Dylon? Isn't he supposed to be helping?"

"He's cleaning the kitchen as they cook your lunch." She avoided his eyes and stared at the ground. "We know how you hate a messy house."

"Mr. Voss employs his own pack to clean, which helps the kids save money to go to a college of their choice." Mr. Rhodes' proud smile spoke volumes.

We walked past the girl into a living room that had glass windows for walls. A set of double doors led to a large back porch that was probably just as big as the house itself. A huge swimming pool sat in the center, and it had a glass floor jutting over the cliff's edge. You could swim to the edge and look over it to the beach below.

Several tables and chairs were arranged around the pool, all wood with light beige colored cushions laying on each chair.

"Please sit." Mr. Voss moved over to a section that held a large table with eight chairs. Of course, he took one of the seats at the end.

"This is amazing." Simon glanced around with a huge smile on his face. "Now, you've only recently become the city alpha, right?"

"Yes, he came to me several years ago, asking for me to be his mentor." Mr. Rhodes smiled so proudly, much like a father looking at a son. "And here we are, history in the making."

"What do you mean history?" Liam frowned. "We haven't heard anything about this."

"You don't need to." Simon lifted his nose in the air. "It's our area, but if you must know, Mr. Voss was a pack alpha's son, who has worked hard and risen up through the ranks."

"Yet, you have a problem with a woman doing it?" Why was I not surprised after he was cool with the way Mr. Keith treated females?

"Yeah, females aren't made to lead." Simon laughed, and the other two alphas joined in.

"You have to be able to take what you want, and women can't do that." Mr. Rhodes shook his head. "They're always too caught up in their feelings."

"Maybe they can think of the consequences more thoroughly?" Evan arched an eyebrow.

"Overthinking is for the weak." Mr. Voss lifted his head as the wind blew through his hair. "We need action-oriented leaders who aren't afraid to make a decision at a moment's notice."

"Quick action sometimes is a bad decision." Liam shook his head.

"Please, don't." A girl's screams came from the house. "Just let me go."

"Ahhh... There she is." A cruel smirk filled the alpha's face.

"What happened?" Mr. Rhodes arched an eyebrow.

"One of my girls turned eighteen today and thought she could run away without my permission." Mr. Voss licked his lips as he paused. "She hadn't worked like the other pack members to request such a thing, so we had to bring her back."

"What are you going to do with her?" Micah's golden eyes darkened.

"Well, I finally found a woman that is almost my equal as far as females go. She has a hunger like me but for her freedom." Mr. Voss chuckled as two large guys dragged out a girl who was digging her feet into the ground. "It'll be fun to break her and let the other packs watch as it happens. You know fear is the best way to keep them all in line."

"No." Her long blonde hair was a tangled mess as one of the men used it to grip her head, both eyes were blackened, making her jade irises somewhat dim. Her arms had deep claw marks from where they must have fought her in wolf form.

My stomach dropped. He was going to beat her.

"Why can't she have any freedom?" Simon's voice was slow and very controlled. "It's obvious she doesn't want to be here."

It took a second for me to process what he'd actually said. It had even taken Evan's head snapping in Simon's direction to finally allow the words to sink in.

"If you start letting people have choices, it only encour-

ages others to act out. Your father shares the same senti-
ment, so I'm surprised you're questioning this." Mr. Voss
stood and sauntered over to her like she was the prey. "I told
you running would do no good, Sherry."

We can't let this happen. No one deserved to be broken.

No, we won't, but we do have to be smart about this one.
Liam reached over and squeezed my hand under the table.
This is Simon's territory, and his dad is crazier than he is.

Yeah, that sounded par for the course.

"Oh, she is a pretty one." Mr. Rhodes nodded in
approval. "Is this the one you're considering to bond with?"

"Yes, but I'm still not quite sure." Mr. Voss shrugged his
shoulders. "It'll depend on how things go tomorrow, I
suppose."

A low growl escaped Simon, and he stood on his own
two feet. "You can't beat people and force them into a bond
that they don't want."

Evan glanced at him with his brows furrowed.

I'd never seen this side of Simon before. Maybe we'd
finally found a line he wasn't willing to cross. I had been
beginning to wonder if one actually existed. *Something is
going on with Simon.*

Yeah, I have no clue what it is. Liam stared at his friend
with narrowed eyes. *I guess physical abuse is where he
draws the line.*

That's not true. Flashes of my brother tied to the tree
sprung to my mind. Simon had beaten my brother to lure
me after Liam finally submitted to our bond. He had even
tried to kill me.

"I can do whatever I want." Mr. Voss placed a finger
under Sherry's chin and forced her head up to look him in
his eyes. "Go take her to the guest room and lock her up. She

needs to be in tip-top shape so everyone can see how I break her."

"Yes, Sir." One of the goons nodded as they forced her back inside the house.

Simon slammed his hand on the table and took a deep breath. "She's injured. She needs food and water."

"No, it'll help the display tomorrow. Make her even weaker." Mr. Voss sat back in his seat and winked at Simon. "Besides, she'll be worse off tomorrow than she is today, so if she's not a hundred percent, it'll still work."

The rest of the afternoon dragged on as Simon stayed silent and kept glancing in the direction of the house where they'd taken the girl. For once, maybe he and I would be on the same page. There was no way in hell that alpha was going to touch her.

CHAPTER NINETEEN

W hen we arrived at the Four Seasons, Simon was still preoccupied. He hadn't spoken more than a few words since he saw the girl being abused. He kept chewing on his bottom lip and was jittery.

As we rode the elevator to the top floor, uncomfortable silence descended among us. Simon had demanded his own room this time, which was odd. He had been the one who wanted to share a suite with the other two, afraid that we might exclude him from something.

The five of us walked out of the elevator and went to our assigned rooms. Evan and Micah were still sharing one together since they had a two-queen bed option.

As soon as we got into our room, I took a deep breath as I took it all in. The room felt exactly the same as all of the others we'd stayed at. The sheets were white and the carpet a tan that complemented the dark wood of the table and dresser. A tan couch sat in the corner of the room.

I made my way over to the couch and sat. "We have to save her." The city alpha was using her as an example, and I could only imagine what would come of that.

"We will." Liam put our bags on the floor by the dresser and joined me. "Every region is messed up. If these big cities that get a lot of attention are corrupted, there is no telling what we could find elsewhere." He ran a hand down his face and sighed. "If I hadn't seen all this shit with my own eyes, I would have a hard time believing it."

"How come?" That was something I was struggling to understand from these four men. They grew up with their parents, and hell, it was clear they were assholes.

"Because we were taught never to question them." Liam chuckled, but there wasn't a smile on his face. Feelings of regret coursed through our bond. "I mean, they raised us to be just like them, and everything made sense... until you." His eyes landed on my face as a tender smile spread. "You made me realize that there was something more to me than some jaded, arrogant man."

I leaned over and pressed my lips to his. *You are so much more than that, and I'm glad you're starting to see it. All four of you are. You don't have to be your fathers.*

I realize that now, and it's so damn freeing. He leaned back and glanced at the clock. "It's getting late. We need to rest so we're ready for tonight."

My stomach rumbled as if proving his point. "Let's get some room service."

"Good idea. We're going to need our energy tonight." Liam took out his phone and began pressing buttons. "I'm texting Evan and Micah to see if they want in on helping us tonight."

"What about Simon? Maybe we should mention something to him." He had acted compassionately earlier, so I hated to make him feel excluded. I was learning that it was one of his triggers for acting out. He was very much like a child; attention was attention even if it was negative.

"He's a wild card, but I'll call his room and feel him out." Liam wrapped an arm around my shoulders and shook his head. "Sure, something actually may have appeared to bother him today, but one phone call from his dad, and it all could change."

That's true. Even though we took his cell phone, now that he was alone he could call his father from the hotel or one of the alpha's houses. "You know if we do this and don't include him, he's going to go crazy for two reasons." I turned my body toward Liam. "First, every time he feels excluded, he gets progressively worse; and two, this is his region."

"Which is even more of a reason I don't want to bring him, but given how he's been acting, you might be right. He may deserve a chance." Liam took a deep breath. "I hate that there is so much between us now. He and I were the closest out of the four of us growing up, but something changed in him. I have no clue what. It's like he's willing to do whatever it takes to impress his father."

"We all have our secrets." I knew that better than anyone else.

His phone buzzed with a reply from Evan.

"Sounds perfect." I brushed my lips against his.

"Let me call Simon and fill him in." He dialed the number to Simon's room and then threw his cell phone on the table. "He didn't answer, thank God." He grabbed my waist and pulled me into his chest. *We haven't had any time together over the last few days.*

We've been busy. I opened my mouth, letting his tongue slip inside. It felt like ages since we'd been together like this.

I climbed on top of his lap and relished the feeling of his hardness against my core.

You're killing me. He pulled back and grabbed the edges of my shirt, pulling it over my head. He dropped it to the floor, and his eyes roamed over my body. *You're so beautiful.* He circled his arms around me and removed my bra, staring at my breasts. *So damn beautiful.* He lowered his lips to my nipples and began to suck and bite.

My head felt dizzy, and I grabbed his chin, bringing his lips back to mine.

He growled as he stood up, my legs still around his waist as he placed me on the bed. I slipped my fingers along the waistline of his slacks and unbuttoned them, dragging them, along with his underwear, to the floor.

Not wasting any time, he unbuttoned my jeans, removing the last two barriers between us before his fingers slipped between my legs.

"No, wait." I pulled his hand away, yanking his shirt off him and throwing it on the floor. I kissed his lips, moving down his neck to his chest.

You're making me crazy. He grabbed my waist and spun me around so I was facing the bed.

As I leaned over the bed, he slipped inside me with one hard thrust. Soon our bodies were in sync, and he hit all the right places like never before. It wasn't long until my pleasure started building, and he leaned forward, placing his fingers between my legs, and rubbed.

I wasn't sure how many times I rode the waves of pleasure, but when he began digging deeper against me, I knew he was getting close to his release as well.

He increased our pace, and soon the friction started building once again. Right when I thought I couldn't take it any longer, we both climaxed as one.

When it was over, he kissed my back as I stood and turned toward him. My stomach growled loudly, which caused a huge smile to spread across his face.

Liam leaned over and kissed me again. "Let me order some room service. We can't have you hungry."

SIMON HAD DISAPPEARED, and we didn't have time to wait on him. So the four of us left without him. We took a cab but had them stop a few blocks away from the gated community. We had to act now. Luckily, the gate was only for traffic in and out and did not extend through the actual forest. It made sense that his pack would want to run in the open.

We had to be careful not to run into any of his pack. Luckily, it wasn't a full moon, so most of them wouldn't be out and about.

We had been dropped off at a bustling street near the beach where we could shift and run up the huge hill to get to the alpha's house. A strip mall sat across the street along with several bars. Because of the amount of traffic there was, we decided it would be easier to hail a cab and prevent the pack from chasing us outside the woods.

Liam took my hand and pulled me toward the trees.

"We're good. No one is paying attention." Evan's voice was only a whisper, careful not to alert any of the humans to our plans.

"Let's go," Liam said as we rushed to hide behind the closest set of thick trees.

Once we were in our natural element and hadn't raised any alarm, my heart began to beat steadily again.

Liam's eyes glowed in the darkness. "I'm going to stay human since we will need to be able to get through the gate and into the house and still be able to communicate. You three can shift."

I looked around as my eyes adjusted and took a deep breath, enjoying the hint of saltwater in the air. I dropped my backpack on the ground and nodded over to a small opening about ten feet away. "I'm going over there to shift." The last thing I wanted to do was get naked in front of Micah and Evan, and it would be a good spot to leave my backpack. I'd packed an extra set of clothes for each of the guys and the girl, too, so that once we got here, she could shift back to her human form.

Not wanting to waste time, I ran over and quickly removed my clothes, shifting onto all fours. When I ran back out to the others, they were there waiting for me. Micah's wolf was the darkest of the two while Evan's fur had a reddish tint, which matched his auburn hair.

Liam made his way to me and dug his fingers into my fur. *You'd better be careful. I don't like you being here with us, but it'd have been worse if I left you behind.*

Everything will be fine. He has no clue we're coming. I couldn't promise it, but I needed him to calm down and focus on our target.

The four of us glanced at each other, and we took off toward the houses.

Has anyone heard from Simon? It shocked me that the heirs hadn't heard from him. He didn't answer earlier when Liam tried calling, but I had expected to see him before heading out this way. Also, we needed to keep an eye on him, but tonight this had been more important. I only hoped he didn't mess this up somehow.

No, it's odd. Evan ran by his room quickly when we were heading out, but he didn't answer then either. Liam took the lead, moving fast but carefully since none of us knew the surroundings. He let his wolf out just enough to keep his pace the same as ours.

The hike up the cliff was longer than I realized, but it was nice to run, letting my animal loose. It had been far too long in my human skin, and being in my fur was invigorating.

The four of us ran together in unison until we noticed the tree line growing a little thinner. Liam slowed the pace as we surveyed what was in front of us.

Our main problem was that the four of us weren't a pack, which was becoming more and more frustrating the longer I got to know them. Only Liam and I could communicate, but that was due to our mate bond.

Light allowed me to see someone moving from the corner of my eye and the scent of another wolf shifter hit my nose. *We're not alone.* I took another deep breath and couldn't believe my nose. The smell was fruity. Uh. *It smells like Simon.*

A low growl emanated from my chest as I turned to stare at the one person I hadn't expected to find. My nose had to be playing tricks on me.

Don't move. Liam's voice was commanding as if I would actually listen. *I'll be there in a second. There's no telling why he's here.*

I trotted over as Simon's eyes caught my own.

"Of course, you'd be here." Simon rolled his eyes as he stared at me.

"What the hell are you doing here?" Liam said in a quiet voice as he appeared beside me. "You're going to get yourself killed."

"This is my region." Simon lifted his head as he watched the other two heirs catch up in their animal forms. "And why am I not surprised they are here too?" He sighed.

"Well if you aren't worried, then why the hell are you

sneaking in just like the rest of us?" Liam arched an eyebrow and crossed his arms.

Simon closed his eyes and took a deep breath. "Because I'm here for the same damn reason you are. I can't sit back and let him hurt her."

"Really?" Liam waved his hands toward the houses that we could see in the distance. "Why?"

"I don't know why." His face scrunched in pain, and he shook his head. "But I can't let her stay in there. Dammit." He ran his fingers through his ash blond hair and pulled at the ends. "It doesn't make any sense, but I need to save her, and that douche wouldn't be willing to hand her over. So here I am."

"We're trying to get a feel for what's going on and figure out which room she's in." Liam pointed over to the city alpha's house. All the lights were off downstairs, but there were a few rooms lit on the top floor.

"She's in the corner guest room." Simon pointed at the room that was closest to us, which overlooked the woods. "He has her tied to the bed so she can't escape."

"How do you know this?" Liam's brows furrowed.

"When I went to use the restroom while you all ate, I watched his two idiots leave the room and saw her right before the door shut." Simon lifted both hands in the air and shook his head. "She looked so damn weak."

She's his mate. That was the only thing that made sense. Simon was torn up right now and even more angry at the fact that he was upset.

Yeah, I think so too. Liam's face remained neutral as the two men stared each other down. "Then, why don't you join the four of us to save her?"

"I need to stay in human form to remove the rope." He

pulled out a knife from his pocket. "But you four can cover my ass."

Of course, this had to be about him and his ego, but having two people in human form would be a good thing. Sometimes, it was an advantage to remain on two legs.

"Fine. That way, at least we can all be on the same page, but," Liam said as he narrowed his eyes at his friend, "don't do anything stupid. I'll override you in a heartbeat."

"I won't. We can't risk getting caught." Simon's eyes, for once, weren't crazed; they were full of determination.

Liam must have found whatever he was looking for because he nodded. "I'm staying in human form too so we can all communicate."

"Fine." Simon rolled his eyes.

The five of us were quiet as we carefully hurried through the rest of the woods, bringing us close to the city alpha's house. The closer we got, the slower we moved, watching for anything that seemed out of sorts.

Right as we reached the edge of the tree line, I glanced around but didn't see or smell anyone outside. The moon hung high in the sky, alerting us to the fact that it was approaching midnight.

We trotted to the back of the house and ran to the gate that led onto the porch where we had spent the afternoon.

Simon grabbed the top of the privacy fence and pulled himself over, landing on the other side. Within seconds, we heard a slight click, and the gate slowly opened without a sound. Liam grabbed it and waved the three of us in to join Simon on the other side.

He quietly shut the gate as we entered the backyard, and all of us paused as we glanced around, waiting for something. The water of the pool rippled with the breeze, and the sky was eerily quiet.

"It's clear." Simon's words were like a faint breeze.

I could barely hear them. As we all quietly moved to the back door, Simon pulled out a knife and started messing with the lock.

What the hell is he doing? We were going to get caught. We hadn't thought out all of this.

No, he knows what he's doing. Liam's eyes met mine. *He broke into his dad's car and hot-wired it when we were sixteen.*

That was something I hadn't expected.

Within seconds, the back door unlocked, and Simon opened it just enough for all of us to fit through.

"Micah, stay here, and keep an eye out." Liam glanced at his friend. "Alert us if anything happens."

The dark brown wolf nodded his head as he moved to the side of the porch where he blended in with the shadows. His gold eyes were the only indicator he was there.

"Come on." Liam waved Evan and me inside the house after Simon. Once the four of us were inside, he closed the door just enough that it appeared shut even though it was still barely open.

I searched for any signs of someone downstairs, but luckily it was dark and quiet. It sounded like there was a television on upstairs, which I thought may be a blessing to help drown out some of the noise.

Simon scurried across the living room and turned left, heading into a small walkway with its door shut. He turned around and pointed at the door.

This is where she is. Liam linked with me.

I wanted to be a smartass to him, but now wasn't the time. He was only stating the obvious.

Once again, Simon worked the lock with his knife, and

it only took moments before he opened the door and slipped inside.

Evan stayed outside to guard the hallway as the three of us slipped inside the room.

I paused when I saw the girl on the bed.

Her head jerked in our direction, and I noticed that the circles under her eyes had become even darker than when we last saw her. Her legs were tied to the footboard, and her arms were tied to the headboard. The ropes didn't have any slack in them, not even to move an inch. There was duct tape on her mouth, but her jade eyes widened in horror.

"It's going to be okay." Simon walked over and held the knife in his hand.

She whimpered and tried jerking away from him but with no luck whatsoever.

She thinks he's threatening her. Simon wasn't the comforting type.

"He's not going to hurt you." Liam lifted both hands in the air as if he was proving that Simon was trying to be helpful.

"Shh. Be quiet," Simon hissed as he went to work, sawing at the ropes. "You two are going to alert the house that we're here." He'd finally cut in through the first rope, and she had one arm free.

As he moved to the rope holding her leg down, she used her free hand to rip off the tape.

Her eyes widened as she took all of us in. "Who are you?"

"We're here to save you." He released the rope from that leg and moved to the other side to work on freeing her other leg and arm. "The less you talk, the better."

"Okay, but we need to hurry. His beta and third in command come in here frequently to check on me. They're due any second now. I'd thought you were them." Her voice was low, but it was filled with so much damn hope.

A tingle ran down my spine. *Do you hear anything?* It was as if her words made the air seem different.

It'll be okay. Liam tried to reassure me, but his words fell flat. *It's just our nerves.*

In what was probably only seconds but felt like minutes, Simon completely freed the girl, and she jumped onto her feet. "We have to hurry now."

She rushed past us as she rubbed her wrists and headed to the door. When her eyes landed on Evan, she came to a complete stop.

Simon ran toward her and grabbed her arm. "He's with us. Let's go to the back door." He mouthed the words as he pointed to the back door.

He kept his hold on her and tugged her out the back door as the rest of us followed close behind. When he turned to shut the door, the living room light turned on, and one of the idiots caught our scent. He looked right in our direction, locking eyes with Simon.

"Shit, go," Simon growled as Micah jumped to his feet, rushing to the gate with the five of us.

Liam hurried forward and threw open the gate as we all ran desperately to the forest.

A loud howl filled the air, and the back door flew open with a crash.

We weren't getting out of here without a fight.

CHAPTER TWENTY

You take Sherry and run. Liam's voice was a loud command in my head. *You two get down there and in human form; mix with the crowds. They won't be able to get you then.*

That was the one most important rule of any wolf shifter and the shifter world. Humans weren't allowed to know of our existence.

"Simon, let her go with Mia." Liam glared at his friend as if daring him to disagree.

"Fine." He took a deep breath and looked at Sherry. "Go with her." He pointed at my wolf. "I'll follow the others to you."

The girl paused for a second as she looked at him. "I... I don't want to leave you."

"It'll be safer if you go." Simon's body sagged as he stepped into her. "I promise I'll be there as soon as possible."

You'd better run with us. I didn't want to leave Liam. Not here. *We all need to run together.*

The girl took in a deep breath, and more wolf howls

filled the air. She took off after me as the guys followed several yards behind.

As we ran through the trees, I could hear several footsteps getting closer and closer. They knew the woods and had the advantage. I didn't think we were going to make it without joining the fight.

A brown wolf appeared to my right, his eyes locked on the girl we'd saved. A deep growl emanated from his chest, and his entire focus concentrated on her, not me. He dug his paws into the ground and jumped, obviously hoping to sink his teeth into her arm. He wasn't trying to kill her, just capture her.

I stood on my hind legs and steamrolled him directly in the side, causing him to fall hard to the ground and roll over.

A loud howl filled the air as his focus moved to me. He bared his teeth at me, and saliva dripped from his mouth. He crouched low on his legs and began to sprint straight at me.

Considering how fast he was moving, he was hoping to dominate me with his strength. I had to counter his move but couldn't immediately or he'd have time to fix his aim to my chest. At the last second, I jumped back, making him stumble and fall at my feet.

The last thing I wanted to do was hurt him, but he was already scrambling to get up.

I had to prevent him from getting to Sherry. I jumped on his back right before he stood and sunk my teeth into his shoulder.

He started bucking, but I held on tight, sinking my teeth in as deep as they would go. He rushed to a tree and stood on his hind legs, knocking my body hard into the bark. My breath left me.

Mia, I'm on my way. Liam's voice filled my head, and I could feel his panic through our bond.

A light blonde wolf flashed before me and raced for the wolf that was smashing me into the wood. It took me a second to comprehend that it was Sherry.

Her teeth sunk into the wolf's uninjured shoulder, and he landed back on all fours.

I dropped to the ground and took a deep breath, which hurt like hell. I must have bruised a rib or something. As I took in a smaller breath, I realized the brown wolf was now going straight for her neck.

Dammit. I forced myself to my four legs and launched onto the asshole's back. I clawed his back, trying to cause him pain. Hoping that somehow, he wouldn't be able to focus on attacking her neck.

The wolf groaned as I thrashed his skin with my nails. Blood seeped from the wounds, coating his fur.

He started backing up to a tree again, obviously hoping to make me release my grip on him once more.

Sherry rammed him hard in the side, making him stumble and hit his head on a thick branch.

He collapsed to the ground and passed out.

Now that she and I both were in animal form, we couldn't communicate. I took a deep breath and jerked my head in the direction we'd been heading. *We're fine. He's passed out.*

Good, then run. A few more are heading your way. Liam growled through our bond. *I'll be there as soon as I can.*

Sherry and I took off again, running as fast as we could through the woods. We were making good time until pain broke through Liam's and my bond.

I stopped in my tracks and turned around. I couldn't keep running away when my mate was injured.

It took a second for Sherry to realize I'd stopped, but when she did, she turned around and caught back up. She motioned with her muzzle in the direction we'd been running, but I shook my head no. I couldn't keep going.

I heard growls and picked up the scent of blood. They were getting close. I took off in the direction of the smell, and it only took a few minutes before I came across the four heirs fighting six wolves. Now Liam and Simon were both in their wolf forms. However, they were outnumbered.

My heart slowed some when I saw that Liam was fine. He was fighting a wolf almost as large as him and was holding his own. One of the wolves that had been fighting Micah turned and focused on something behind me.

The wind had shifted, and Sherry's scent hit me before I even turned my head. No, she'd followed me back here.

The wolf left Micah and growled, alerting the other five to Sherry's presence. One of the two that had been fighting with Evan wandered over too. They growled as they approached her, focused only on getting her back to the city alpha.

As the first one struck, I launched myself at him and made him tumble to the ground. He rolled over quickly and got back to his feet.

Mia, what are you doing? Liam glanced over at me; his eyes full of fear. *Go to the end of the cliff near where we were dropped off.*

No, you guys are outnumbered. There was no way in hell I was going to leave him like this.

Something sharp bit into my previously injured shoulder, making my eyes water. The second one had attacked me while I'd focused on the other. A whimper left me as blonde fur appeared next to me, biting into the neck of my attacker.

The wolf's mouth slackened, and I was able to free my shoulder without too much damage. Blood dripped down my leg, but I ignored it as the one I'd knocked over began to circle me.

He lowered his head to the ground as he tried to make me feel like prey.

Little did he know; I wasn't falling for it.

I glanced around, and now each one of us was fighting one of the wolves. At least it was a fairer fight.

The wolf charged at me again, but when he was only a few seconds away, I lowered my body to the ground. He stumbled over me, and I quickly lifted my front half up, making him hit the ground hard.

Sherry still had her wolf by the throat as he tried bucking her off him.

The wolf I was fighting stood back up and narrowed his eyes.

Instead of allowing him to be the one to attack, I decided to go all-in. I ran toward him and noticed that his eyes flickered to his left. He was going to try to dodge the blow. At the last second, I turned my body to the right and bit into his shoulder, jerking my head left and making a large gash.

He whimpered in pain but took advantage of my neck being wide open and latched onto it. His teeth sunk in, and blinding pain coursed through my body.

I fell to the ground when he didn't let up on his hold.

Mia, dammit. Liam's voice was full of fear, but I couldn't even turn my head to look for him.

Something crashed into us and Liam's scent hit my nose. The wolf's grip loosened on me, and I remained on the ground as I struggled to catch my breath. Liam's teeth dug through the wolf who'd been hurting me, but unlike them, he jerked his head, ripping the wolf's throat out.

The wolf collapsed on the ground and didn't move again.

Are you okay? Liam whimpered as he sniffed around my throat at the blood.

I moved my neck around, and even though it hurt, I could feel my healing already kicking in. *I'm fine. Already starting to heal.*

Good. He licked my face.

Sherry whimpered not far from us, and Simon turned in her direction.

The other wolf had her pinned down so she couldn't move.

Liam rushed over and knocked the wolf away from Sherry's body, allowing her to move out from under him. Liam growled as he lowered his body, pushing his head underneath the wolf and throwing him at least twenty feet away. When the wolf hit the ground, it was with a loud thud, and his head hit a thick branch, knocking him out.

As I turned my attention back to the three other heirs, I realized they were all still fighting, but as Liam, Sherry, and I approached, the other three city pack wolves began backing away. They were outnumbered and severely injured.

Evan growled and charged with Simon and Micah flanking both sides. As they attacked the wolves, they fought for their lives, but the heirs were just too strong. It wasn't long before they turned and ran back to the alpha's house.

As the six of us looked at each other, Liam nodded his head back to the landing. *We need to hurry; they are probably getting others to come back them up.*

I hadn't even thought of that. The six of us ran hard, rushing to safety.

WE HAD to split up between two taxis on the way back. I'd thought the drivers might call the cops when they saw the state we were in. It was a cool night, so we were able to hide most of our injuries with our clothes. However, none of the cab drivers gave us a second look, and we made it back to the hotel with no issues.

Since we were all in an injured state, we took a side door into the hotel and went straight to our rooms.

As we walked into my and Liam's room, the tension was thick amongst the six of us.

"Why did you save me?" Those were the first words Sherry had spoken since she'd escaped the house.

I stayed silent since her eyes were only focused on Simon.

"I..." He blew out a breath and shook his head. "I don't know."

Well, this was going well. "Because what he was going to do to you wasn't okay. It was the right thing to do." He had to realize that they weren't their fathers.

"But why and how?" She glanced around the room, taking it all in. "Who are you guys? You do know he'll come for you?"

"It's not possible." Simon's arrogant tone had already slipped back into place. "And you have to know who we are."

Why is he being that way? He couldn't even blame me for coercing him to go. He was already there by himself.

"We..." Shit, I almost slipped my secret. "They are the heirs of The Blood Council, so he really can't do much."

Remember how I struggled with our bond? Liam worriedly glanced over at my neck. It was beginning to scab over but still hurt. *I guess it's his turn.*

Well, I supposed that made sense. Liam was an ass at first too.

"That doesn't make any sense." She shook her head and worried her bottom lip. "Your father hasn't been concerned with our well-being for a while."

"How would you know that?" Evan's eyes narrowed.

"Because my dad was the city alpha before that asshole took over a year ago." She shook her head and snorted. "My dad was no saint, but he didn't treat his pack members like they were property."

"Really? Where is your dad? Did he step down?" Micah's golden eyes widened as though he was scared.

"No, that prick killed him right in front of my eyes." Sherry's eyes glimmered with unshed tears. "That's how he took the position."

Evan stiffened as he glanced at the door.

What's wrong? Whatever she said had caused alarm amongst them all.

In order to be promoted above your station, you aren't supposed to kill the alpha but let the council decide. Liam pulled his phone from his pocket. *That means that Simon's dad gave him the blessing, which also puts us at risk for Simon's dad to get involved and make us give the girl back. The farther and quicker we take her away, the better.*

"I'll take care of the flight." Evan hurried out our door and toward his room. "We should be ready to take off within an hour."

"Let's get packed and head out." Liam glanced at Micah and then Simon.

"But... our grandparents forbade it when they were on the council." Micah shook his head. "They said we were more civilized than to let our beast take over and inflict pain. It's supposed to be a council decision."

"And who do you think approved it?" Sherry faced Micah; her nose wrinkled in disgust. "Mr. Green approved of having that asshole kill my dad and take over the pack."

"But why?" Something seemed to break inside Micah, and his tone was full of angst.

"We just need to get the hell out of here before Dad gets involved." Simon headed to the door but paused and looked at Sherry one more time. "I won't be long." He took a deep breath and walked out the door.

Once the two other heirs were gone, Sherry turned to face both Liam and me. "I don't know what to say. You two are the main reason I'm here." She blew out a breath and tilted her head. "I guess what I'm trying to say is thank you."

"You're welcome." I smiled, trying to put her at ease.

"Well, I know who those four are, but who are you?" Sherry arched an eyebrow. "Other than his mate."

I liked her. She was direct and to the point. "I'm Mia."

"I'll get out of your way so you all can make it home." She headed to the door. "Thanks again."

"Wait." Did she think we were leaving her behind? "You need to come with us."

"But I don't have any money, and my ID is back with the pack." She shrugged.

"You don't have to worry about any of that." Liam nodded at her. "We'll take you back with us. Get this resolved and figure out the next steps from there."

"If you don't want to stay with us after we get things

calmed down, you'll be free to go." The last thing I wanted for her was to feel trapped.

"And you have my word that we'll help you through whatever decision you make." Liam's eyes glowed with his wolf, sealing his words with a promise.

"Well, okay." She blew out a breath.

Now we had to go back and face the council. I had a feeling they weren't going to be happy with the results from the trip.

CHAPTER TWENTY-ONE

The six of us entered my dorm room, staying away from the men's. All four of their dads had been ringing their phones nonstop once we landed back in town. They'd been notified that their personal plane left early and was headed home. It was after ten in the morning when we finally got back, and Liam figured that their dads would have someone at their doors, waiting upon their return.

They wouldn't expect all four of them to be in my dorm, at least not at first. So we stopped to get Sherry situated before they came knocking on the door.

"After all this time, I'm finally here." Sherry's face was losing some of the bruising, which made her look a lot healthier.

"What do you mean?" She must have wanted to attend Wolf Moon like my brother had.

"With my dad being the Los Angeles city alpha, I was pretty much guaranteed a spot here." She blew out a breath and huffed. "But when he was killed, my future vanished before my eyes."

I hadn't even considered how not only had she lost her

father but her future too. "Well, maybe there is still hope." If Simon didn't reject her, she'd be a shoo-in here.

Liam's phone began ringing again. "Would he just leave us alone?" He pulled his phone out and almost hit REJECT.

"You might as well answer it." The longer they put it off, the worse it would be. "They know we're here." The guard had checked us in.

"Fine." He pressed the ANSWER button and put the phone on speaker. "Hello."

"Liam, it's about damn time that you answered." Mr. Hale's voice was angry with possibly an edge of hysteria to it. "You and the others are to report to the council room here on campus at once."

"Fine, the four of us will be there soon." Before he pressed END, his dad cleared his throat.

"Son, you better bring *her* too." Mr. Hale's voice was full of hate. "She's the problem anyway." The line disconnected.

"You're not going." Liam shook his head as he headed to the door.

"No, I am; they want me there." I glanced around the dorm and noticed Bree's luggage in the corner. I hadn't expected her to come home yet. "Bree?" I took a deep breath, but her scent wasn't heavy in the room. She had to have left the house at least an hour or so ago.

"She's not here?" Evan hurried through the living room and turned down Bree's hallway. He knocked faintly on the door. "Bree?"

Silence was the only response.

"What am I supposed to do? Especially if your friend is here." Sherry glanced around the room, taking it all in.

"Hang out in my room." I pointed down the hallway next to us. "Bree won't bother you there." That probably wasn't true, but at least Sherry wouldn't be just hanging out in the living room by herself. "If you do see her, just tell her you met us while traveling and came back to tour the school."

At least, that was believable.

"Maybe she should come with us too." Simon stared at her like he was afraid to look away.

"Having her go with us would be a horrible decision." Liam's brows furrowed, and he shook his head. "Honestly, I wish Mia would stay behind."

"They're going to try to scare us, aren't they?" Micah took a deep breath as if he was preparing for battle.

"Yeah, they are." Simon ran a hand through his hair. "And dammit, I don't know what the hell to do." He stomped his foot on the floor.

At this very moment, he reminded me of a toddler throwing a temper tantrum.

"We go in and stay united." Liam glared at Simon. "Do you get it? If they think we're fracturing, they'll try to divide us even more."

"But..." Simon lifted a hand in the air.

"There aren't any take-backs." Evan's voice was deep and low as he stared Simon down.

"What the fuck is that supposed to mean?" Simon had that crazed look in his eyes that he got when he felt like he was losing control or things were changing.

"He means you helped us with her escape," Liam pointed at Sherry, "and we didn't force you. It's time for you to stop dancing the line and finally pick a side."

"But they're the members of the council." Simon pointed at the door. "We can't go against them."

"We already have." Micah huffed. "So, you need to own it and move forward. Otherwise, you're essentially giving her back to that city douche." Micah nodded his head in Sherry's direction.

"Fine, let's just go." Simon turned toward Sherry. "Are you going to be all right here for a little while by yourself?"

"I don't think I have a choice." She shrugged as a yawn overtook her.

"My room is the door down this hall." I smiled at her. She had to be tired given how much healing was going on in her body. "You can even lock the door and take a nap if you want to."

"But it's your room."

"No, it's fine. There are towels in the bathroom, and you can wear whatever you want from my closet. Go relax and get comfortable. We shouldn't be gone that long.'

"Fine." She smiled at me. "Thank you." Then, her eyes stopped on Simon. "Are you coming back too?" She reached over and touched Simon's arm.

He jerked back like her touch stung. "Uh... yeah." He winced as if it pained him to say it. "I'll be back with them."

"Uh... okay." Hurt flashed across her face as she walked down the hall and into my room.

"Let's go." Evan rushed out the door and toward the elevator. The four of us followed behind.

It didn't take long before we were walking across the campus toward the gym where the council worked on the top floor.

"What do you think they're going to do?" Micah's body was tense, and worry lined his face. "They can't really do anything, can they?"

"No, here in the next year, they have to hand the council over to us." Liam took my hand in his and pulled me next to him. "A council can't rule longer than twenty-five years. This year will be the end of their reign."

When we reached the building, Evan yanked open the doors, and we all piled into the elevator. Within minutes, we were out of the elevator and walking into the council room.

The room wasn't what I had expected. The walls were blood-red, and the silver curtains pinned to the sides of the windows allowed a lot of light to enter the room.

There was a large wooden table in the corner where four chairs were placed on one side. Each council member sat in one, and we faced them head-on while standing.

Mr. Hale and Mr. Rafferty sat in the two middle seats with Mr. Green next to the eastern alpha and Mr. Croft on the other side of Liam's father.

For a moment, the nine of us were staring each other down. Once again, it struck me how their fathers looked so young. It didn't make any sense.

"Is there anything you'd like to tell us?" Mr. Rafferty arched an eyebrow as his focus landed on his son.

"Oh, yeah." Simon lifted a hand as he pointed at the council. "We decided to come home early. Hope you don't mind."

"Is this some kind of joke to all of you?" Mr. Green's eyes widened as he gaped at his son.

"Nope, not at all." Simon smiled at his dad. "We met some people, took in the sights. Did you know that California's cool in the evening this time of year?"

"Aw, man." Micah chuckled and shook his head.

"It's cool in the evenings all year round." Mr. Green's face turned a shade of red. "You grew up there."

Mr. Hale slammed his hand on the desk, cutting straight to the point. "We'd expected your trip to be a memorable one, and this one most definitely was but for all the wrong reasons. Now we'll have to fix everything you messed up."

"I disagree with you." Liam released my hand and took a step in front of me. "We met with each regional and city alpha and learned all about the welfare of our people."

"Your trip wasn't meant for you to learn about their welfare." Mr. Rafferty's voice was so angry, it was almost a rumble. "You were there to meet the leaders and see the sights."

"In other words, it was supposed to be a superficial trip?" Micah snickered, but there wasn't a smile on his face.

"Oh, come on, Son." Mr. Croft's skin matched Micah's. His eyes weren't golden though but black. There was a cunningness to him that Micah didn't have. "This was just a political move to get you out in view of the packs. There was nothing more to it than that."

Mr. Rafferty stood and leaned over the table. "All you had to do was play the part like we raised you to do."

"But Dad, we saw people living and working in horrible conditions ... women being abused." Micah took a few steps toward his dad as if he was delivering unknown horrible news.

"Enough!" Mr. Croft yelled, effectively cutting off Micah from saying anything further. "That is none of your concern."

"Like hell, it's not," Simon said as he moved to stand beside me. "We deserve to know everything. It's pretty damn clear that you've been keeping secrets from us."

Never in a million years would I have expected Simon to be on the same page as the rest of us, but here he was, standing strong next to me.

"We have a right to know what we're getting into when we step into our roles." Liam arched his eyebrow. "And I pray to the gods that none of you had a clue about how our people were being treated."

"Our people?" Mr. Green asked as he stood and began laughing as if he was a madman. "You've got to be kidding me. They're our servants, doing whatever we tell them to do."

When he did that, I realized how similar he and Simon looked. Simon looked like a slightly younger version of his father.

"Whether you like it or not, we will be ascending the council within the year." Liam stood tall and glanced at each one of the council members.

"You still have much to learn, Son." Mr. Hale's words were harsh. He stood, moving around the table and heading straight to Liam. "And I expected so much better from you than this. There is only one person that I can think of who would be the cause of it. Hell, she manipulated you to take her on the trip after I told you specifically not to." His eyes landed on me.

"I wanted her there. So, leave her out of it." Liam's voice turned deep with rage.

"Or what?" Mr. Hale shook his head as he wrinkled his nose in disgust. "I told you she would make you weak, and now look at you."

"He hasn't become weak at all." Evan crossed his arms as he stood next to me. "Maybe you were afraid she'd open our eyes to what you're trying to hide."

"What? Let me guess, she's your mate too." Mr. Rafferty snarled at his son.

"No, she's a friend." His jaw twitched as he ground the words out.

"That's even worse." Mr. Rafferty's face filled with such hate. "I've taught you to be strong."

"Your version of it." Evan dropped his hands to his sides.

"Is this what you really want?" Mr. Croft arched an eyebrow at his son. "For a girl to come between us?"

"It's more than that." Micah's forehead lined, and he looked at his dad like he was someone he didn't know. "Not only did she save my life, but I saw how mistreated our people are out there. It's not good to turn a blind eye to it."

"You will do what we say." Mr. Green lifted his head, looking down his nose at us. "That's how it's always been and will continue to be."

"What are you so scared of?" I should have been quiet, but these were the assholes who'd killed my father. And now they had the audacity to threaten my mate and friends. "That they will stop listening to you or become more than you?"

Mr. Hale reared his arm back before launching it right at my face. Before it could connect, Liam caught his hand, preventing it from hitting its intended destination.

"You will never do anything like that ever again." Liam's eyes glowed as his wolf took over. "If you think our relationship is strained as it is, the next time you try something like that, I won't think twice about hurting you."

"You value her over me?" Mr. Hale tried pulling his hand from Liam's grasp, but he couldn't.

"Hell yeah, I do." He dropped his dad's hand, causing him to fumble a few steps back. "If you want us to be the doting heirs we've always been, then you need to stop this charade. Whether you like it or not, you need us."

"Maybe we don't." Mr. Green bared his teeth at us.

"What would happen if all the packs learn that the heirs weren't interested in taking over the council?" I was playing with fire. "There is already civil unrest out there, do you need to stoke the flames even more?"

The four members grew quiet as my words sunk in.

We turned to leave, but I stopped before I reached the door. "Oh, and we have a new student who needs to be enrolled tomorrow."

"No." Mr. Hale ground out his words.

"If you want to keep up appearances, it'll happen." Simon nodded at me. "The ball is in your court."

"Dammit." Mr. Rafferty picked up his chair and threw it against the wall.

"Fine." Mr. Hale's eyes met mine. "I hope you realize what you're doing." He glanced at the heirs. "What you all are risking ... all because of her."

I hoped we did too. Something was going on here even though I wasn't sure quite what.

"I don't think there is anything left to say," Evan said as all four guys surrounded me, and we walked out of the room together.

As we exited through the building, my phone dinged. I pulled it from my pocket and saw a message from Bree.

Hey - Meet me out in the clearing behind the education building. We need to talk where there are no prying ears.

"I need to go meet your sister." It was a strange request. We normally met in our dorm.

"Well, it could be a trap. We're going with you." Liam turned around and faced the others, waiting for a challenge.

"Sherry is back in your room." Simon glanced at the girls' dorm.

"She's safer up there hidden than out here potentially in sight." Liam patted Simon on the shoulder. "And they know we won't behave if they act out right now."

"Fine, but it has to be quick," Simon growled.

The five of us stayed in human form as we rushed to meet Bree.

As we drew closer to the clearing, I felt something buzzing in the air. Something I couldn't quite put my finger on. "Do you feel that?"

"Feel what?" Liam squeezed my hand, which he was holding in his.

"There's an energy in the air." It was as if the air was rubbing my skin, causing friction to fizzle throughout my body.

"I don't feel anything." Liam glanced around.

"You know how the air charges right before a lightning storm?" That was the only way I could explain it. "The air feels kind of like that now."

"I don't feel a damn thing." Simon glanced up, looking at the sky. "And I don't see or hear any lightning."

"Dumbass, she was trying to explain it." Micah chuckled. "She wasn't saying it was about to storm."

"Maybe it's your nerves, Mia," Evan said, but he winced like he didn't believe his own words.

We stepped into the clearing, finding Bree in the center alone. She turned and crossed her arms. "I didn't expect to see all five of you here."

"We're kind of a package deal now." Simon shook his head. "I'm not sure if I like it though."

"I wanted to talk to you, but maybe it should be another time."

The friction seemed to be getting worse, but I tried to focus on my friend. "No, it's fine. They can be trusted."

"Even Simon?" Bree furrowed her brows.

"He's fine." Liam took a deep breath. "What is it?"

"I was asked to come here on behalf of the rebellion."

Bree straightened her shoulders as she said the words clear and slow.

"Is this some kind of joke?" Liam narrowed his eyes.

"Maybe our fathers are testing us." Simon spun around, looking for a sign.

"No, I went back to Nate's home, and his pack isn't doing well." Bree took a deep breath. "And ... I learned that most packs aren't doing well. I decided to take a stand, and Mia, they want you to stand with them too."

"You do realize you're asking us to betray our families? All of us." Evan's voice was slow and clear as if he was trying to make her think it through.

"I do, but our dads aren't following through on their oath." Bree lifted her hands. "There are people without homes, people whose children get taken away from them, and even people who can't eat. It's getting worse and worse over time. We have to do something."

The air was charging even more, and at this point, I was in pain.

Mia, what's wrong? Liam turned to me with so much concern in his eyes.

I... I don't know. I focused on the air and began moving with it toward whatever source it was rushing from.

"Mia?" Bree yelled after me, but I couldn't stop.

The five of them followed me as I walked through some trees.

"No, we can't go in there," Micah yelled at me. "It's off-limits."

Even though I heard his voice, my legs were now moving on their own. I climbed over the chain fence and hopped down on both feet. Something kept pushing me forward.

The five of them caught up to me as I stepped into

another small clearing. Right in the center was a cement circle that was at least twenty feet around.

"What the hell is this?" Liam glanced around.

"I don't know." But I was determined to find out. I walked straight to it as the energy increased and circled the area.

"I feel it now," Evan said as he walked around the clearing, scoping out the area.

My eyes landed on the design that was drawn into the cement. It was the same one that was on my pendant. Four silver paw prints, and on top of them was one paw print drawn in red. "It's the original council's emblem."

"Holy shit." Simon's eyes widened as he saw it too.

"What have our parents been up to?" Micah searched for something in the air as if the energy was so thick it should be visible.

"Whatever it is, it's definitely not good. This energy doesn't feel natural." I glanced at Bree. "I'm in. I'll join the rebellion."

The four of them nodded their heads as well.

"We're in." Liam glanced at his sister. "What do we do next?"

A huge grin spread across her face as she said the next words. "Get retribution."

We were going to war, and finally I'd get all of my answers even if it killed me.

The End

ABOUT THE AUTHOR

Jen L. Grey is a *USA Today* Bestselling Author who writes Paranormal Romance, Urban Fantasy, and Fantasy genres.

Jen lives in Tennessee with her husband, two daughters, and three miniature Australian Shepherd. Before she began writing, she was an avid reader and enjoyed being involved in the indie community. Her love for books eventually led her to writing. For more information, please visit her website and sign up for her newsletter.

Check out my future projects and book signing events at my website.
www.jenlgrey.com

ALSO BY JEN L. GREY

Wolf Moon Academy

Shadow Mate

Blood Legacy

Rising Fate

The Royal Heir Trilogy

Wolves' Queen

Wolf Unleashed

Wolf's Claim

Bloodshed Academy Trilogy

Year One

Year Two

Year Three

The Half-Breed Prison Duology (Same World As Bloodshed Academy)

Hunted

Cursed

The Artifact Reaper Series

Reaper: The Beginning

Reaper of Earth

Reaper of Wings

Reaper of Flames

Reaper of Water

Stones of Amaria (Shared World)

Kingdom of Storms

Kingdom of Shadows

Kingdom of Ruins

Kingdom of Fire

The Pearson Prophecy

Dawning Ascent

Enlightened Ascent

Reigning Ascent

Stand Alones

Death's Angel

Rising Alpha